I don't mean to sound ungrateful, because I know that I'm blessed, but it's like I worked hard my whole life to get here and for what? I busted my ass and got good grades, and played the part to every teacher and boss I ever had because somewhere along the line someone told me if I just followed the rules I would be rewarded with a sense of satisfaction. That I'd be happy...But I'm not, and I don't know how to be.

ZLS
New York California

Flawed Hap/iness

Copyright © 2015 by Cori Tadrus

Published by Lusory Books. An imprint of ZLS Publishing

All rights reserved. No part of this book may be reproduced, stored in a retrieval system or transmitted in any form or by any means without the prior written permission of the publishers, except by a reviewer to be quoted and printed in a newspaper, magazine or journal digital or print. For information, please contact: ZLS Publishing in writing at

> ZLS Publishing
> 1425 Central Avenue
> Suite 5074
> Albany, NY 12205
> or visit our website at:
> http://zlspublishing.com

This is a fictional book. The entire book, from the front cover to the back cover is 100% fictional and is a figment of the author's imagination. Names, characters, places, things, and incidents are either the product of the author's imagination or are used fictitiously, and any resemblance to actual persons, living or dead, businesses, companies, events, products, or locales is entirely coincidental.

The publisher does not have any control over and does not assume any responsibility for author or third-party websites or their content.

Cover design by Vann Taylor

Printed in the United States of America

10 9 8 7 6 5 4 3 2 1

ISBN 978-0-9845986-2-5

Library of Congress Control Number: 2015934998

Learn more about the author by visiting her at: www.coritadrus.com www.facebook.com/coritadrus, and https://twitter.com/CoriTadrus

Dedicated to my husband, Dave, and my daughter, Eva, for your unending patience, support, and love.

"It is the very pursuit of happiness that thwarts happiness"-Viktor Frankl

Table of Contents

Prologue

7

Chapter 1

Am I Happy?

23

Chapter 2

What's Gonna Make Me Happy?

37

Chapter 3

Happiness at a Sportsbar?

57

Table of Contents

Chapter 4
Happiness at a Holocaust Museum?
85

Chapter 5
Happiness Amongst the Naked?
115

Chapter 6
Happiness In a Taxi?
143

Chapter 7
Happiness in Cancer?
169

Chapter 8
Finally Finding Happiness
201

CHAPTER 1

Lately, every day brings nothing but the usual. The usual irritating chime of the alarm clock; the usual cup of lukewarm coffee with amaretto creamer; the usual work assignments, obligations, or errands; and at days end, the usual struggle to locate my apartment keys at the bottom of my shoulder bag. They are being especially obstinate today, so I shake my bag fiercely until the jangling metal ring loops around my desperate fingertip.

I unlock one, two, three locks - click, click, click - and am immediately hit with the smell of my apartment: cardamom and antique wood. Sighing deeply, I kick off my red-soled stilettos, push on my slippers, and head to the kitchen to reheat last night's Indian food from the place around the corner that my mother says, with her authentic blend of grief and guilt, "I spend more time doing business with than any available man."

While the microwave is going, I pull back my hair, light every candle I own, and scroll through the docked iPod, not knowing what I am looking for until I find it. Mr. Stevie Wonder's "As" seeps into me as I shuffle across the walnut plank floor, and fall into the deep tufted leather sofa with my dinner. Watching steam rise off the container of chana masala, I find myself wishing this heavy feeling that has become a part of the usual, would lift from me as freely.

Lately, I just do not feel like the Athena I am supposed to be. Maybe because I turned thirty out of what seemed like nowhere last year, or that I have been single for I do not even remember how long anymore. Or maybe my mother and father, who are Greek-American and African-American, respectively, set the bar a little too damn high when they named me after the goddess of wisdom. Whatever the reason, I am thankful my girls, Nadine and Lori, are coming over tonight. They are always good for some levity and wine.

Just as I am about to send a text asking where they are, Lori taps on the door.

"What the hell took you so long?" I complain while kissing her cheek. Her Halle Berry do is windblown, and the only makeup she is wearing is robin egg blue nail polish, and a shade of fuchsia lipstick that looks gorgeous against her sand-colored skin. She smells of jasmine oil that, just like her, has a sweet and earthy essence.

"The hot yoga studio locker room is being remodeled, so I had to run home to shower. Girl, you would not believe the amount of negative energy your body can exude through a good sweat. Anyway, I also made a stop on the way here, which I'm sure you won't mind." She reveals what looks like a bottle of red wine from behind her baggy tank top, but has the words "malt beverage" on the label.

"You know I don't," I reply. "And I don't care if your cheap butt bought it from the bodega down the street again, either."

Lori cuts her almond-shaped eyes at me. "Now, how are you going to call me cheap, Miss Never-Pay-Retail?"

She is right, I do like a bargain, but that is only because I have expensive taste and could not afford half of what I own by paying sticker price. Whereas Lori just does not like to spend money, even though she earns a good living working as a lab tech supervisor at a major medical center in the city.

We met two years ago through Nadine, Lori's cousin and my oldest friend, when Lori moved to New York from a small town in Ohio to be with her online love, now husband, Michael. They live in Sunnyside, Queens, which is only a twenty minute ride on the 7 train to my Murray Hill, Manhattan loft. Nadine and her husband George also live in Queens, in Astoria, where they own a small accounting firm and where her and I both grew up. Nadine's family moved in two brownstones down from mine when we were five years old, and we have been inseparable ever since. We were even roommates in college.

Anyway, despite the fact that Lori is cheap, and we have not known each other long, she is that friend who would spend her last dime to bail me out of jail, no questions asked. Nadine, on the other hand, would be sitting next to me in the cell, and be the reason I was there in the first place.

"Fuck these mother-fucking stairs," Nadine wheezes, as she appears at the bottom of the flight of stairs leading up to my fifteenth floor loft.

"Obviously a good sweat does nothing for her negative energy," Lori whispers to me.

When she reaches the top, Nadine wipes beads of water off her forehead and adjusts her black lace bra, visible through her neon mesh shirt. She puts an arm around each of us to catch her breath.

"And why are you so late?" I ask.

"Well if your damn elevator wasn't broken again, I would've been here a half hour ago. And I'm sorry, but you know I can't leave the house without making sure George is fed and the kids have had a bath. That man cannot be trusted to wash his own fucking ass, let alone two others."

"Nay, you have such a dirty mouth, but I love you for it," I say, then kiss her cheek. "I'll grab the glasses and meet you ladies on the balcony. Hopefully, it's cooling down out there. I can't believe we're having a heat wave in late September."

"I can't believe with what you pay to live in this old-ass building, you don't have central air or a working elevator," Nadine says.

"It's called vintage and I think it's charming," Lori tells her cousin.

"Of course you do," Nadine says sarcastically, then declares, "Damn, Athena, you're going to burn this place down with all these candles. You expecting a guest later? Oh, now, why do I ask questions I already know the answer to? You haven't had a man in here since your father helped you move in six months ago. And did your dinner come out of that cardboard container on the coffee table? Maybe if you learned how to cook a meal you'd have visitors more often. I'm just saying."

"Since when do I need a man to light candles? Candles relax me. And since when did you become Betty Crocker, Nay?" I yell from the kitchen. "I seem to remember a certain someone existing on Lucky Charms and Ramen."

"First of all, bitch, Ramen noodles are delicious." Nadine's husky voice travels easily through the apartment. "And we were in college! Not all of us had scholarship money and could afford Starbucks and sushi. Plus, I was too busy with extracurricular activities to cook."

"Is that what you call what went on after Freshman English in Professor Watson's station wagon?" I say while sliding open the squeaky screen door with my elbow.

"That man was a freak." Nadine has a far off look in her eye as she smoothes her silky extensions.

I hand them each a glass, and Lori snaps the plastic top off the bottle. "Oooh, your finest crystal," she teases as she fills her glass to the top. "Why do you have such nice things that normal women have to get married and register for?"

"Because I, unlike yourselves, do not need a ring on my finger to justify treating myself to the finer things in life. And, please, I know I'm going through kind of a dry patch—"

I ignore Nadine as she mumbles something about a drought.

"—But I am in no mood to discuss men tonight."

Lori throws up her hands in mock frustration. "Fine, fine. I guess we should talk about other things sometimes anyway."

"Yeah, you're right," Nadine says. "Lor, whatever this is that I'm drinking, it's awful! Oh, and speaking of fine things, Athena, have you *introduced* yourself to that hot new piece of ass at work yet? Don't think I didn't see him last time I came to get you for lunch."

"That's not changing the subject, Nay. But exactly what hot new piece of ass is she referring to?" Lori asks.

I had been waiting for Nadine to bring up Anthony. I know nothing about him except that he has an amazing sense of style, and was hired to replace our former staff photographer, Virginia. I knew nothing about her, either, except that she sat at the cubicle adjacent to my office every Tuesday and Thursday afternoon, listening to Alanis Morissette's *Jagged Little Pill* on repeat as she edited photos and ate sour cream and onion chips. She also refused the Altoids I offered her on a very regular basis. Not sure what the girl had against men or mints, but let's just say I was not sad to see her go.

"He's the new photographer, I haven't even met him yet," I reply. "And see him, Nay? You practically violated the man with your eyes! If I didn't know any better I'd say you were the one not getting any, but I have heard marriage will do that to you..."

Nadine holds up her finger and swallows her sip. "Well, you didn't hear that from me. George might not be the handsomest man I know, the most in-shape man I know, or even the best accountant I know, but he does know how to satisfy his woman."

"Oh please, Nay, stop with that. The last thing I want to think about is George's roly-poly belly bouncing up and down, and you screaming out every four letter word in your vocabulary!" Lori says, exchanging a horrified glance with me.

Nadine sucks her teeth. "Whatever, Lor. All I'm saying is that we should be living vicariously through our single friend over here. She should be hitting all the hottest clubs, with the hottest men, telling us the hottest new positions they've invented since we are committed to one penis for life. Athena hasn't even been on a date since she and what's-his-ass broke up, and that was what, over a year ago?"

She is referring to Damon, the smooth-talking, cocky Dominican with eyes as piercingly blue as a swimming pool on a sweltering summer day. I dated him exclusively for a year, and he dated me exclusively for a month, at best. We moved in together after dating only a few weeks, but his career as a talent agent caused him to be on the road, as well as on young actresses, constantly.

I suppress the nauseous feeling that accompanies my recollection of him and respond, "So not true. Did you forget that guy I met online a few months ago? I couldn't figure out why he wanted to meet up at four in the afternoon until we got to Perkins..." I pause for a reaction "... and the waitress pointed out the 'early bird' section of the menu. The man grinned at me like we had hit the damn food lottery. Then, during our meal, he told me he had just gotten tested for STDs and asked if I knew what that involved for guys. An explanation I begged through a mouthful of soggy onion rings not to hear. But, oh, did he go into gross detail. The word 'swab' makes me gag to this day."

"Hold up. You ordered onion rings on a date?" Nadine asks.

"It was Perkins, girl. What else was I supposed to eat? You know I'm a vegetarian. Besides, I wasn't planning on kissing his raggedy, chapped lips. Anyway, after I paid the check because I couldn't stand to sit there for one more minute while he detailed, ironically, every bad blind date he had ever been on, he proceeded to invite me to his place to watch a movie and then remembered he had sold his TV to make rent, but I was still more than welcome to come sit on his love seat."

Lori covers her mouth so she won't spit out her drink. "Oooh, now I remember that guy! We winked at him because his profile said he was six foot and a professional athlete."

"He was five-two and a mascot. And that's why I don't date online."

"Or at all," Nadine adds.

"Listen, it's cliché, but true. There are millions of men in this city. *But,*" I hold up three fingers, "weed out the few attractive, employed, and *somewhat* decent ones in their thirties, and most of them are either married, gay, or living in their parents' basement in Staten Island, and if that's the case, I've already dated him. Twice."

"That is true," Nadine and Lori say in unison. "However," Nadine continues, "one bad date and you deprive yourself of being wined, dined and grinded, and us the privilege of hearing about it. Athena, I know you are a big fish but this is a big pond. You can't stay single for the rest of your life just because you've had a few – okay, a lot – of bad experiences."

"Yes, I know that. You sound more like my mother every day."

"Leave her alone Nay," Lori says. "Athena's twin flame is out there, the universe just hasn't united them yet."

"Thank you, sweetie. And this is the last thing I'm going to say on the subject. I am keeping my mind – my heart, even – open to romance, I'm just done seeking it out." I top off everyone's glasses. "Really, are we done now? I don't know why three mature, worldly women have to consume themselves with the opposite sex. Honestly, if I can't satisfy myself, and no Nay, I don't mean in that way, how's a man going to do it?"

Nadine cocks her head and Lori sighs slowly, her tucked lips revealing she has had something on her mind for a while. "Well, now that you mention it Athena, what is going on with you? Your aura's been bleak for months, ever since your twenty-ninth... wait, how old are you? Did we celebrate your twenty-ninth birthday two years in a row?"

"Yup, and I'll be turning twenty-nine again on my next birthday." I tip my glass at her and before Lori can finish her thought, Nadine interjects.

"Frankly, you've been bringing us down lately. Half the time you don't want to leave your apartment to go out with us at night, unless it's work related, and you always have this depressing ass look on your face. I don't get it. Girl, you have a wardrobe, a career, and a loft that, besides the cost of rent in this uppity neighborhood, any woman in her right mind would kill for! So, what's the problem? Why aren't you happy?"

My heart sinks under the weight of her words. I had no idea my feelings were so obvious. Pondering my response, I stare between the high-rises across the street at the lights atop the Chrysler building, until they blur.

"Honestly," I say without diverting my gaze, "I'm not sure what the problem is. I guess... the question is... when did this become *'it'*?"

"It?" Lori asks.

"Yeah, 'it.' Life." This doesn't seem to be a good enough explanation, so I think for another moment. "Like in high school, freshman year. On any given Friday night, Nadine would come to my house for a 'sleepover,' then try to convince me to sneak out my bedroom window with her. While she was off partying and hooking up with boys, I stayed tucked in my bed with a pile of books, stressing over college entrance exams that were two years down the road.

"Not to take anything away from you, Nay. I always wished I could be more like you. Living in the moment, but I was always ten steps ahead of myself, and stuck in my own head. Had to be perfect at something or it wasn't worth doing. I went from valedictorian to summa cum laude to grad school to crappy internship to entry level to columnist to finally being able to pay back my student loans to –" I catch my breath. "Lonely.

Unfulfilled. I mean, yes, I have an awesome job and a nice apartment and designer clothes, but at what point did I stop being Athena and start being just the sum of all these parts?" I look into my friends' puzzled faces, halfheartedly expecting an answer, and slink into a heavy sigh when I do not get one.

"I don't mean to sound ungrateful," I continue, "because I know that I'm blessed, but it's like I worked hard my whole life to get here and for what? I busted my ass and got good grades, and played the part to every teacher and boss I ever had because somewhere along the line someone told me if I just followed the rules I would be rewarded with a sense of satisfaction. That I'd be happy... But I'm not, and I don't know how to be." I finish the rest of my drink in one big gulp.

Nadine frowns at me, and sets her glass down with attitude. "Athena, being perfect ain't got shit to do with being happy. Want to know why I'm happy? With my mediocre house, boring ass job, and husband and kids who I love to death but drive me fucking crazy? Because I try to be. I *try* to be happy. It's like... having an orgasm. Just because you're doing what you're supposed to be doing to have one, i.e. having sex, doesn't mean that you will. You can't just lie there, going through the motions and expect it to happen to you. You have to try, Athena.

"Change positions if the way you're doing it isn't getting you off... I mean, damn. There are a whole lot of people in this world that have a lot less than you, but still manage to be satisfied with the little they do have. You need some perspective, sister. And for the record, I really *don't* think a man can fix this," she adds while waving at my head, "but I do know that you have to do *something*, or you will never be happy with anything you have, no matter how great it is."

I crinkle my nose and nod slowly as Lori reaches out to softly touch my knee. "Nadine's right. Happiness isn't something that happens to you. Happiness is something that's within you, and we all have different ways of getting in touch with it. Like, I know you think I'm all new age and granola, but yoga helps me to find my center and achieve a higher state of consciousness. It allows me to see things clearer, to appreciate the good and dismiss the bad in my life. With clarity, there is bliss." Nadine rolls her eyes and Lori holds up her hand. "Some people use spiritual practices or religion. Others," she nods at Nadine, "use sex –"

"It was a metaphor, heifer."

"Seriously, Athena, I think even though it's going to be difficult to find what brings you in touch with your happiness, it is out there. I mean, I knew you were a unique soul from the moment we met. I knew it right after I moved to the city and Nadine introduced us over lunch. Here you were, having just come from the shooting range, wearing six-inch stilettos, leather from head to toe, and insisting the restaurant make the French onion soup vegetarian for you. I didn't know whether to be more impressed with your outfit or the 9 mm peeking out of your Louis Vuitton. That poor waiter was so scared he didn't even charge us for our meal."

"That was not on purpose," I say with a smile.

"I know," Lori replies. "Sweetie, your contradictions are what I've always loved most about you. So, what I'm trying to say is, why should your answer be easy when you are so *wonderfully complicated?*"

"I have no idea. But girl, you are wise beyond your years."

"I know. All twenty-nine of them."

We share a laugh, then sit in silence for a minute, listening to the sounds of the city below. I let my friends' words resonate while they start chatting about a Morris Chestnut movie they recently dragged their husbands to, the plot pertaining to a jaded thirty-something professional woman seeking what else but love and happiness, and then rejoin the conversation by, bringing up the fashion atrocities of last Sunday's Primetime Emmys. We gossip about that until Nadine's phone goes off.

"You have *got* to change your ring tone! *Soul for Real*, for real?"

"Yeah, Athena, George is my candy coated... well, something. He likes candy. And I told you girls he can't handle me leaving him alone with the kids. Look at this text, 'where are the Band-Aids and flashlight?' That can't be good."

"I need to get home to Michael, too. He gets nervous about me riding the subway this time of night. Especially if I've had a drink or two."

Nadine snorts. "No one wants to go near you with that mess on your breath. You could set someone on fire by breathing in their general direction," she says, while doing a breath check on herself.

"Anyway, I have the car so I can give you a ride, but if you ever bring that nasty drink around again, you're on your own."

I walk them to the door, blowing out candles as we go. "Well, thank you both for coming over and listening to my pathetic whining."

Lori embraces me tightly, then cups my head in her hands. "You are not pathetic. Just... intricate. Immaculate, even. A goddess queen."

"Oh lord, she is drunk," Nadine says. "Time to go. Goodnight Athena, I love you. Think about what we said, please."

"I love you both, too. And I promise, I will."

CHAPTER 2

The dusty light of morning trickles in through the space between my oversized velvet curtains, lifting my heavy eyelids from a deep sleep. Such a deep sleep. As my eyes come into focus, I study my surroundings – the crystal tear drop chandelier above my bed; the dried bouquet of white roses from Lori's wedding on top of the distressed dresser; the ornate silver frames on the wall holding pictures of my friends, family, and dream destinations clipped from the pages of *Condé Nast;* and the medallion throw pillows stacked meticulously on the hope chest at the foot of my wrought iron bed.

There is an archway, but no door separating my bedroom from the rest of the loft. It is a wide-open space that I designed exactly like the showroom floor of the Pottery Barn on Broadway, where I bought all this stuff the day after I moved in. Everything except for the bedroom furniture and cedar armoire being used as an entertainment center – I inherited those pieces from my grandmother. It cost a small fortune to decorate, even with the floor model discounts, but it was worth every penny. There is something blissful about having a space that looks and feels exactly how you want it to.

I remember the weekend is not here quite yet, and, pleased to have woken up before the alarm clock, I reach over to grab my phone off the night stand. It is only 7:02 a.m., so I can take my time this morning.

I hit play on my iPod and sing along to Mary J. Blige's "Take Me As I Am," while I am in the shower. After finger-styling my soft, thick hair into loose waves, and putting on a light dusting of shadow and mascara that can easily be made into smoky eyes should a happy hour opportunity arise, I slip into my favorite ivory silk cami, a blazer, skinny jeans, and new knee high camel boots that I have been dying to show off at the office. It is casual Friday after all.

I browse through the *New York Times* online edition as I sip my coffee filled exactly halfway with amaretto creamer, grab a protein bar, and by 8:07 I am out the door. The weather is finally starting to cool, so I decide to forego the subway and walk the eight blocks to work. Something I have not done for weeks now because of the oppressive heat. Today feels different, like autumn has finally arrived to Manhattan. Bright gingers pop off bouquets at the flower stand, and the scent of apple fritters sizzling in a breakfast food truck temporarily replaces the less desirable aromas of the city.

Whether it is from the change of seasons or a good night's sleep, I feel different today, too. I find myself walking a bit lighter this morning, despite the designer leather stretched tightly across my calves and the arches of my feet. I shift in my boots and ponder this change in my mood, as well as my decision to walk to work today. Yes, today, of all days, and when I am breaking them in, as I ride up to the thirty-sixth floor of One Chelsea Centre, home of *The Manhattan Socialite* magazine (or "The Socialite" as everyone calls it). I must admit though, they do look fabulous.

The elevator door opens and Mark, the receptionist also known as my best work friend, raises his thinly plucked brows at me. He cups his hand over his headset and mouths, "Those boots are fab-u-lous."

"I know!" I mouth back as a smile creeps across my face. Wow, I do feel good today. It is almost an uncomfortable change of pace, I think, as I set my shoulder bag under my desk. Having my own office is one of the luxuries of being a full-time staff member here, where my time is divided between writing *The Scene,* a weekly column in the magazine, and the nightlife news blog on our website.

The blog, which details city bar and nightclub openings, closings, and events, and includes a touch of my own commentary, is kind of a pain because it involves constant updating. However, most of the material comes to me via emailed press releases or the occasional phone call from a manager or promoter, so there is little effort on my part to research content. Plus, it provides me with the information needed to choose the hottest spots to review in my column, and what's even nicer for a writer in this city, the means to earn a steady paycheck.

I have no messages to return, so I shake my mouse until the black screen fades to the generic island scene. I was reprimanded by my boss Brian last month for having a David Beckham underwear ad as my wallpaper, which makes absolutely no sense since it appears in almost every issue of *The Socialite.* Some nonsense about "maintaining a professional workspace." I wonder how professional Brian's workspace was when, according to Mark, he was "bumping uglies" with one of his many female interns on his desk during an after-hours strategic planning session. Whatever.

And then there was... "the incident." An image so immensely disturbing it has been burned into my brain for the last two years. It was my first week at *The Socialite,* and I was still a bit naïve to the nuances of Manhattan's underground club scene. An email from an anonymous sender provided me the address and secret password to a "leather and lace party." It was invite-only, and I was not allowed to bring a guest. The girls warned me that it sounded risqué, but, blinded by the excitement of being privy to a secret party, I did not listen.

That night, wearing a knee-length black lace dress and red leather heels, I gave the password through a rectangular slot in a studded metal door. When the door opened, it took my eyes a moment to adjust to the black lights and realize that the bodies gyrating to the deafening techno music were not, in fact, dancing. The last thing I saw before turning around and running out of there was a bare chested man wearing tight leather shorts, a lace mask across his eyes, and snapping a bullwhip. On his head of dark, wiry hair, glowed a lone strip of white. Now, I never found out the source of that email, but one of the only people I have ever met with a mallen-streak in their hair is Brian.

Pushing that thought out of my mind for the 538th time I begin the task of looking busy. *The Socialite's* blogs have been under construction for a few days now, which enabled me to submit my column early this week: a review of a new gay nightclub in Hell's Kitchen called Guy Bar. Nadine is still mad that I dragged her there under false pretenses. So, the only real work I have to do today, besides brainstorming next week's column, is to appear as occupied as possible until 4:56 rolls around. An acceptable time, I have decided, to leave the office. As if we are on that psychic friends tip, my BlackBerry rings and it is Nadine.

"I'm so glad that you called. I need you to go with me to the opening of a new lesbian hotspot on Eighth and –"

"Fuck you, Athena, I still can't believe you took me to that place. Like taking a supermodel to an all-you-can-eat buffet. I couldn't touch *nothing*. Thank God people know you and give you free shit or it would have been a total waste of an evening."

"Okay, okay, I said I'm sorry. Mark had plans and I wanted company. But I don't know what you're talking about because your old married ass can't touch nothing anyway. Regardless, you'll be the first to know if the *Chippendales* come to town, I promise. What's up?"

"Just wanted to see if you're down for cocktails after work with me and Lori. I know you don't have a date or anything, and you probably don't feel like it, but I figured, as a formality, I'd ask anyway."

My first instinct is to decline, but then I remember the comment Nadine made last night about me not going out much anymore, except for when I am in work mode. "You know what? I think I will meet you out tonight. I'll see you at the usual spot around five thirty," I say.

"Well, good. See you then. And make sure you tell *The Socialite's* newest hire that Nadine says heyyy."

"See you later, freak." I hang up the phone, shaking my head. She never stops.

As my mind drifts back to last night's conversation with the girls, melancholy smacks into my chest like an emotional boomerang I cannot seem to throw away. I slink back into my swivel chair and wonder, *"What is it going to take to make me happy?"* Not like the unusually good mood I was in this morning until this very moment, but truly happy.

Instinctually, I turn to Google for help. I type in the word 'happiness,' and the first thing that pops up is its definition.

Happiness:
1. The quality or state of being happy.
2. Pleasure; joy; fulfillment.

I click on the last word, and its definition appears.

Fulfillment:
1. A feeling of satisfaction at having achieved your desires.
2. The act of consummating something like a desire or promise.

The act of consummating? Does even Merriam-Webster have to rub it in my face that I'm not getting any? Although the first answer is interesting. "...*At having achieved your desires.*"

I create a new document and title it *My Desires*. I number it from one to ten, then stare at the white screen blankly until Brian raps on my open office door. I look up, startled.

"Hard at work, huh? Sorry to disturb you, but wanted to give you a heads up about something." He closes the door behind him, and sits across from me with a look of intensity and excitement on his square face. He picks at his untamed eyebrow with two pointy fingernails as he speaks. "I'm announcing a new idea for the magazine today during the writer's meeting, something I've been sitting on for a while now, and finally feel ready to move on. There will be a lot of changes around here, and since your column is one of the most widely read, I need you on board."

"On board for what?" I ask.

"Well... for example, there are dozens of publications in the city that review the 'grand opening' of this' or the 'under new ownership' of that, but I want to take you-take-us, to a higher level. Stand out among the crowd."

"How?" I am very uneasy with where he's going with this.

"I want to get more creative. Dig deeper. I want you to be less Sarah Jessica Parker and more Dorothy Parker." He lingers on this phrase, waiting for a reaction from me, which I refuse to give him.

"Anyway, we'll talk details in the meeting. I'm glad I have your support, Athena."

With that, he scurries out the door. *What just happened?* I reach for the phone to call Mark.

"Hey," I whisper into the receiver, for no apparent reason except for effect, since Brian closed the door behind him. "Brian just came in here talking about making some big change around here. He's going to make the announcement at the writer's meeting today. What have you heard?"

"Big change? Sorry, I'm out of the loop on this one, honey. But you better let me know as soon as you find out what it is."

"I will," I say, still whispering, "but you've lost major street cred here. Thanks for nothing." I hang up, and glance at the time on the bottom of my computer screen. Another two hours until the meeting. My mind starts racing with possibilities.

'Stand out among the crowd?' 'Dig deeper?' I mean, what the hell could Brian be thinking? I review nightlife for *The Socialite*, not political strategy for *Newsweek!* Not to mention, I get VIP treatment at every hot spot in the city. I *cannot* and I *will not* go back to being one of those sad looking people behind the velvet rope. It took a lot of work to get where I am, and I like it here. I do not want to dig anywhere!

A dull ache swells between my temples. I take a deep, calming breath and tell myself not to get all worked up. Brian said he wanted to *change* my column, and that could mean anything. Maybe he just wants more words or bigger words or bigger celebrity sightings; I could do that. I mean, who knows if it was Jared from Subway or really Justin Timberlake licking salt off a pair of gigantic breasts during tequila fest at Southern Hospitality. It is always dimly lit in bars. However, he did say something about creativity, and coming from Brian, that is the part that scares me.

With my stomach still doing cartwheels, I stop torturing myself and turn back to the document I parked at the bottom of my screen before I was so rudely interrupted. "My desires... My desires... My desires," I say out loud, looking around my office for something that will inspire a thought. Nothing. I finally spot the latest issue of *Bazaar* sitting in the stack of mail on top of my bookshelf – which holds every issue of *The Socialite* that's been printed since I have been here, in chronological order – and start typing:

#1. This season's Gucci bag
#2. A six-figure salary
#3. Someone to grow old with, who, preferably, also wears Gucci and earns a six-figure salary
#4. To have every day be a good hair day
#5. For Brian to not mess with a good thing

Reviewing my list, I realize it looks more like what I would wish for when rubbing a magic lamp than a means to feeling complete. So, if achieving a desire is not the same thing as having a wish come true, maybe it is more like reaching a goal. Though, I have achieved a lot of the goals I have set for myself. Like graduating a year early, being debt free by the time I turned thirty, and losing that extra ten pounds I was carrying around after Damon and I broke-up (rocky road, like my ex, did not love me back). Still, something is missing. There has to be more to it. Damn being complicated!

My head feels like it is about to implode, so I give up on the list for now, and do some aimless YouTube-ing until it is time to hear the news I have been spending the morning trying not to speculate about. I grab my protein bar and head to the conference room, just as Mario, the delivery guy from Fat Boys Deli, is setting up the courtesy lunch they send up from the ground floor every Friday. I am the first one here, so I take my usual seat as the smell of day-old pastrami sandwiches fills the room.

On his way out, Mario, who smells like a day-old sandwich himself, leans over to me and mutters through his missing front tooth, "So, when are you going to let me take you out, sexy?"

"I tell you every week Mario, I'm not."

"And you have yet to give me one good reason why not?"

"Well, I just… don't like meat."

He laughs perversely as he exits, and I realize that comment probably bought me another two years of harassment. Great.

As the additional eight members of the full-time writing staff file into the room and take their sandwiches and seats, Brian goes to the front to write four words in big red letters on the dry erase board – *Souls of the City*. After doing a roll call into the speaker phone to ensure all the contributing writers are conferenced in, he shoots me a look — as if we share a big secret that is about to be revealed – that I am sure everyone catches, considering their confused expressions.

"Good afternoon everyone. Before we get into the specifics of the next issue, I have an announcement." Long pause. "As you all know, *The Socialite* has been one of the most widely circulated local periodicals throughout the boroughs since its inception in 1981. For over three decades, we have been the voice of what's hot and what's not in New York.

"People love us, trust us, and most importantly, pay us to tell them where to go and what to do in this amazing city of ours. There are plenty of free publications that do exactly what we do, only we do it better. The reason we do it better is, besides having the advantage of bigger advertisers that finance a bigger budget, we possess that illusive, intangible, invaluable thing called an 'edge.'

"But an edge only lasts as long as the status quo does. Fortunately, or unfortunately for us in the literary world, things are moving at an unprecedented pace. Every major publication is now online, which is why we launched our website ten years ago. To stay ahead. Think about it this way: if you have a computer or smartphone, which nearly everyone does these days, you have access to the opinions of every self-professed expert and critic out there.

"My grandmother even has her own blog where she blacklists businesses that don't offer senior discounts. It's pretty funny, by the way. You should all check it out. Anyway, the point is, in order to maintain our edge, we need to give people what our competition, which is now the entire World Wide Web, doesn't, and that's the human element. That's... a little something called 'soul.'"

I glance quickly around the table, and see a lot of bodies shifting in their chairs. Everyone seems to share my cynicism.

"The printed word still has one advantage over the cyber one. Accountability. Printed on every issue is an address where New York writers come to write New York columns. Our readers know you and feel like they have a relationship with you because you are real people who breathe the same polluted air, ride the same subway system, and have the same frustration with tourists as they do. They know this because we are there, just as *The Socialite* has been for the last thirty-two years, to give them exactly what they want, what we have told them they want, without fail, in their mailbox or neighborhood newsstand every single week. Everyone follow?"

We all nod slowly in agreement.

"So, how do we improve on this edge? How do we build these relationships so that our readers don't get bored with us and go running to another publication, or to Yelp, or to grandma's blog?

"I return to my point about the human element. What we do know about our readers beyond their demographics? What do they know about each other? Who are the people who go to the theater... concert... retail establishment... restaurant... and art exhibit you write about?" He gestures to the respective columnists, stalling lastly at Lily, our art critic, who returns a blank stare.

"Up until now, if we've focused on anyone, it's been, for example, a gallery owner whose one to two paragraph bio reads like a résumé. Yet, who is this person, really? Is he a painter turned businessman due to his wife taking everything, including his inspiration, during their bitter divorce? What about the artists whose work is on display, who are they? Who are their muses? Who are the people who attend his exhibits?

Who are *the souls of the city?"* Brian underlines the phrase written on the board three times as he is saying it for emphasis.

"Starting next week, we are going to begin a piecemeal experiment with our columns. Test the waters to gauge readers' reactions before we do a complete makeover. I've chosen Athena to take the first crack at this, and I've already come up with an angle that lends itself perfectly to her column."

My co-workers turn to look at me as I ask the question I am sure they are all wondering. "What exactly do you have in mind?"

"I'm glad you asked." He flashes a devious smile as if I am playing along as planned. "A six week best-of series called, *Come Here Often*. You'll revisit your favorite places, to be divided into six categories of your choosing, and start by writing about what makes them the best in the city.

"Then, in the second part of your article, you meet up with a patron. Someone who seems interesting. You ask them why they chose to come to that particular bar on that particular night. What about the place attracted them? Are they a regular or is this their first time? Then you *dig deeper*. Ask where they're from. What they do. *Who they are.* Where are they going next? Follow them around for the evening to see how one New Yorker experiences the city on a night out. Go home with them if you have to."

"Do you really think that's safe?" I interrupt, with more brashness than I should.

"No, of course not. You'll need a partner with you, and that's one of the reasons I hired Anthony. For those of you who haven't met our new staff photographer yet, he comes to us from *The R&B Beat*. He made quite a reputation for himself there by capturing the softer, more human side of the musicians he photographed.

"Do you all remember the magazine cover of the rapper that wears all the gold chains, I don't know his name, Lil' something, that went viral a few months ago? The one taken right after his release from prison, where he's holding his newborn baby against his naked, chain-less chest, and there's a tear rolling down his face? That was Anthony's photo.

"So, his task on this project, besides keeping you safe, Athena, is to bring that same level of emotion to the photographs of your subjects. Instead of the standard stock photo of the establishment you review, your column will include a photographic journey of the evening, wherever it takes you."

Brian must have misinterpreted my curious expression because he adds, "Play nice, Athena, I know you're used to working alone. I've already briefed him on everything I just talked about. Since Saturday is your normal night on *The Scene*, you guys will start tomorrow. You should use the rest of the day to figure out your slant on this. After the six week test period is up, we'll review the feedback and decide if the rest of the writers will go in a similar direction with their columns. Athena, I'm counting on you to be our inspiration here. Take this idea and run with it."

"Everyone else, it's business as usual," Brian continues. "I have some things to attend to with the interns so I'm going to end here. If you haven't already turned them in, make sure this week's columns are to editing in the next hour. No need to discuss next week's, you're all brilliant. Have a great weekend."

Brian taps the speakerphone off and with a flash of maroon sweater vest behind him, he adjourns the meeting. The rest of my peers gradually rise and trickle out of the room. No one wants to go back to their desks on a Friday afternoon. I get a lot of raised eyebrows, smiles, and "good lucks" when we part ways in the hallway, and as I turn into my office, Mark's voice is in my ear.

"So? Do I still have a job or do I have to go back to the lingerie department at *Neimans?*"

I spin around to scold him and cannot help but giggle as I see the bra he has made for himself out of cone-shaped water cooler cups and paper clips.

"I told you never to sneak up on me! You know I took Tae Bo in the nineties. Get in here!" I pull him into my office and push the door closed. He has the sorriest look of anticipation on his face. "Wow, it's really killing you that I know something before you do, isn't it?"

"Perhaps. Now spill! What's the big change?"

"First of all, relax. Your job is safe, for now. I would take that thing off, though, before somebody else sees you."

In one quick move, he pushes his chest out – the cups fly onto my desk and the paper clips tinkle to the floor – then he sits in the chair opposite mine, legs crossed and chin in hand.

"Second of all?" I throw the cups back at his head as I take my seat.

"Second of all, the big change is the direction of the magazine. Brian wants the writers to get more personal with our columns. Explore the 'souls of the city.'" I fan out my hands to relay Brian's enthusiasm.

"Oooh, sounds fascinating."

"Yeah, I hate to admit it, but it's not a bad idea. I mean, this could actually be... good. The new photographer's going on assignment with me though, and I don't know how I feel about working with a partner. You know how obsessive I can get about my work."

"Obsessive? That's putting it mildly."

"Well, what do you know about him?" I prod.

"Anthony? Not much, he only started here a few weeks ago. Except, you know, his full name is Anthony J. Blake, but his personnel file doesn't say what the 'J' stands for; he was raised in the Bronx; takes his coffee black, two sugars; wears a size twelve and a half shoe; and rotates his cologne between 'Burberry Brit' and 'Vera Wang For Men.'"

"Oh is that all? Not that I care, but do you think he's gay?"

"Sweetie," Mark huffs, "just because I'm gay doesn't mean I have some kind of magical, omniscient gay-dar. Just because a man has style and takes care of himself doesn't make him a homosexual. Have a little sensitivity."

"Sorry, I didn't mean to be insulting," I respond in earnest.

"Besides, I asked him out a few days ago and he said, 'I'm not gay.'"

Shaking my head, I retort, "You're too much. Don't you have a phone to answer, or a g-string to construct out of office supplies? I have to get to work on this."

"Say no more, I'm gone. Have fun this weekend, don't do anything I want to do," he singsongs, and with a wave he is out the door.

"Wait, Mark?"

"Yesss?" He pops his bead back in.

"What's Anthony's extension?"

"1-2-6-9."

I pick up the phone, and not even thinking dial 126... "Hey!" Our extensions do not go that high.

"It's 1-2-1-6 sweetie!" Mark yells down the hall.

We only have one staff photographer for the entire publication, which explains why I have only seen the man twice since he was hired. I know he has to check in at some point today, so I leave him a voicemail explaining that I got the news from Brian and wondered if he wants to meet up tonight to discuss plans for our first assignment. I give him directions to the bar where I am meeting the girls, and leave my cell number. After brainstorming ideas for tomorrow night until 4:56, then making a quick stop in the ladies room to touch up my makeup, I am out the door.

*****

Nadine and Lori are at our usual high-top table when I arrive at The Bleu Martini Bistro. A dirty martini straight up with two bleu cheese stuffed olives is sitting in front of the empty seat, waiting for me.

"Have I ever told you that you guys are the best?" I say, as I hang my blazer over the back of the stool.

"Yes, but I never grow tired of hearing how great I am," Nadine jokes as she fans herself.

"Athena, are those boots new? They're fabulous!" Lori exclaims as I exaggerate the need to kick my legs while taking a seat.

"Why yes they are, and aren't they?" I take a long sip of the cold, briny drink. "So, to what do I owe the pleasure of seeing you ladies two nights in a row?"

"Well, Michael's out of town on business until Sunday, and Nay conned her mother-in-law into having a sleepover for the kids tonight."

"Nay! Why don't you just hire a babysitter instead of sticking that poor woman with your, excuse me, but brats every weekend.

"Oh, no excuse necessary. They are brats, but who am I to stand in the way of the one thing that brings joy into her old, lonely life?"

I give her a look that says child please.

"Besides, haven't you all ever seen the Jerry Springer episode when the eighteen-year-old babysitter seduces the husband and he leaves his voluptuous wife for her scrawny, no kid-having ass? Uh-uh, not in my house."

"You shouldn't watch that trash," Lori says, and turns to me. "Athena, how was your day?"

"It was pretty interesting, thanks for asking. My column's going to be different for the next few weeks..." I paraphrase Brian's speech, in the middle of which the cocktail waitress brings us another round. "Anyway, I have a few ideas that I have to work out with my 'partner,' which reminds me"--I retrieve my BlackBerry and see that I have a missed call and text from Anthony--"Oh, he's meeting me here in an hour."

"Who's –?" Lori starts to ask before Nadine cuts her off.

"Wait, wait, wait. He? Who's this *partner* that's coming here in an hour?"

"Anthony, the photographer who's working on the column with me. Yes, the very one that you visually raped last time you came by the office. Brian thought I needed a male presence with me so I don't get kidnapped or anything, and supposedly the man has talent. We're going to throw around some ideas tonight."

"Throw around some ideas. Tonight. Here. With Anthony. Huh! And you decided to *o-mit* this juicy piece of information from that boring ass play-by-play of your work day you made me listen to for the last twenty minutes?" Nadine says, her neck snapping back and forth with such force I am surprised it does not snap right off her body.

"Ummm... yes? Can I have another round over here?" I signal the waitress.

Nadine continues. "Let me get this straight. Anthony, the sexy as hell, designer suit and no-wedding-ring-wearing photographer is going to be working closely with you over the next six weeks? Do I have this right?"

"He was probably only wearing a suit because you saw him the day he had his interview."

"So, he's good looking, artistic, and wears designer suits? Athena, you sure the man isn't gay?" Lori asks.

"You know, just because a man has style and takes care of himself doesn't make him a homosexual. Have a little sensitivity, Lor."

"I'm sorry, you're right. Tell us more."

"That's all I know. Like I told you before, we haven't even been formally introduced. This is strictly professional anyway."

"Professional my ass, Athena. The man is single and has such rare, desirable qualities he can be confused with gay. You better go ahead and put some caramel on that hot fudge sundae." Her analogy cracks me up, but she does not crack a smile. "I'm serious, if you don't make a move I will. Married or not, I don't care."

"Oh, yeah right. You talk a lot of shit but we all know George is the apple of your eye. So calm down."

"Don't tell me to calm down. You better do something, Athena. I mean it. Or we are no longer friends." Lori and I laugh at Nadine's empty threat.

"You are such a drama queen. If there's chemistry, she'll act on it."

"Thank you, Lor," I say.

"You will act on it if there's chemistry, right?" Lori asks.

The drinks arrive just in time. I slide both olives into my mouth and mumble while I chew, "Yes, okay, I promise you both that if there's a connection, at that level, I'll pursue it."

"At that level. You kill me, Athena." Nadine picks up her drink and sets it back down with urgency. "What time did he send you that text?"

"I don't know, I didn't ch –"

"Well, he's here."

"Oh God, how do I look, do I need to fix my hair? Shit, do I have olive skins in my teeth?" I run my tongue ferociously from side to side.

"Relax, you look great. Strictly professional, huh?" Lori teases.

"Whatever, just don't embarrass me." I look at Nadine specifically when I say this, and turn around in my chair to see Anthony scanning the crowd.

"This is like some real life Whitney Houston, Kevin Costner, *Bodyguard* shit that's about to happen. I can feel it! And I – I – I – E – I, will always love youuuu!" Nadine sings at the top of her lungs. I want to die.

She is successful in catching his attention, and as I stand up to wave him over, I whisper loudly to Lori, "Take care of her please, or she's the one that's going to need a bodyguard." I must have stood up too fast because I have to grab the back of the chair to keep my balance.

"Athena, right?"

"Yes, Anthony, so nice to finally meet you." I reach out to shake his hand. "These are my friends who were just leaving, Lori and Nadine."

Lori smiles while Nadine, who is just about on top of him, stares.

"Hello," he says, offering her his hand.

"Mmmmmm," is her reply as she leans in to him. I am pretty sure she got a good whiff of his cologne.

"Time to go, Nay. We're going to be late for that thing. Good luck on your session guys." As soon as she says it, Lori blushes and Nadine bursts into a laughing fit. *Kill me now.* Lori finally manages to push Nadine's ignorant ass out the door, and I feel the need to apologize. "Sorry about that, my friend isn't so good with handling her alcohol."

"No need to apologize. Shall we get started?" Anthony asks, as he takes Lori's seat.

Before I can reply, the waitress is instantly on him. He orders his drink, then starts talking about his conversation with Brian. At this point I notice how beautiful he really is. Fresh shaven head, brown and butterscotch eyes with a golden ring around his pupils, a hint of a stubble that's not 4:59 or 5:01 but exactly five o'clock, strong arms, really wearing that shirt, and… "One cranberry juice. With a twist." The waitress pushes her cleavage unnecessarily close to his face as she sets it down.

"Thank you. Um, Athena, you all right? You look a little out of it."

"Yeah, I'm fine. Just haven't eaten much today. You were saying?"

"I was asking if we are on the same page here. Do you want to look at a menu?"

"No, no, it's cool." The waitress sets down a fourth martini in front of me. I do not remember ordering this one.

"So, what I was thinking," I reach under the table to grab the list of ideas that is in my bag, but miscalculate the distance between my arm and the bag, smack my chin on the edge of the table, and fall back and hit my head on the stool.

"Ow," is what I manage to utter, as I hold my head in my hands.

Anthony rushes over to help me up, and in the process, my left elbow catches him right in the crotch. He winces a little, but clearly tries to be a man about it, as I apologize at least five times without taking a breath.

"Seems like you are the one who isn't so good at handling her alcohol. Let me get you, and me, some ice."

He disappears and even though the room is spinning, I swear I catch the waitress smirking at me. Anthony promptly returns with one Ziploc bag full of ice and offers to get me a cab.

"That'd be great, thanks," I say, placing the bag on the growing bump. The cold feels soothing, even though my pride hurts way more than my head.

As he walks me outside, I realize that I did not pay my tab.

"You owe me one," Anthony replies with a wink.

"I think I owe you like fifty." I am trying my hardest not to slur but it is so not working. *How did this happen?*

As I duck into the cab, I ask if he wants to meet at Starbucks in the morning to discuss the column. "I promise I won't spill hot coffee in your lap or anything." "No, I have a lot to do tomorrow, but I trust whatever decisions you make. I'm just the photographer. You have my number on your phone from when I called you earlier, so shoot me a text and let me know where and when we are meeting."

"Okay, I will. Sorry again."

He closes the taxi door and I am left with a bag of ice on my head and fabulous boots on my feet as I ride home alone through the streets of Manhattan.

Happiness At a Sportsbar?

CHAPTER 3

I awake with a jolt as my BlackBerry dances loudly and rudely on the nightstand. I must have switched it to vibrate before passing out. "Hell-lo?" I cackle hoarsely.

"Ooooh, it sounds like someone had a long night! How was it?"

For one glorious moment, my brain does not recall any of the prior evening's events, or why it is throbbing so badly. Then I remember.

"Oh God, Lori, it was mortifying!"

"What was? You didn't have a good time with Anthony?"

"Good time? I hit the man in the nuts!"

"What!? What happened?"

"He was there no more than ten minutes before I made a drunken fool out of myself. I went to get my purse from under the table and next thing you know, I bump my head and then his dick. Only me!" I moan.

"You didn't seem drunk when we left! Then again, you were standing next to Nadine. You know she had two drinks before you got there, but you didn't have that much!"

"I know, but all I ate yesterday was a protein bar and olives soaked in vodka. Three martinis on an empty stomach is clearly a recipe for disaster."

"Did you guys talk at *all*?"

"No." I pull myself out of bed and go directly for the medicine cabinet. The black and white tile floor in the bathroom intensifies my wooziness, and for a second I feel as if I am going to be sick.

"We didn't even get to the column before my smoothness got in the way. I asked him before I left if he wanted to meet for coffee this morning, but he declined. Said something about how he trusts whatever decisions I make. That he's just the photographer. I'm stuck on assignment with this man for six weeks Lor! How am I going to do this?" I shuffle into the kitchen with my three aspirins and crack open a bottle of water.

"I'm sure it wasn't that bad, sweetie. So, you fell. So, you touched his penis, and not in a good way. These things happen! I'm sure even Mr. Designer Suit has imperfect moments. Just laugh it off and show him a fantastic time next time."

"Oooh, if only it were that simple. I'm so embarrassed. I don't know how I'm going to face him."

"You'll be fine. This is strictly business, remember? You're an accomplished columnist who happens to be human. Just be yourself and do what you do best. When do you see him again?"

"We're suppose to meet again tonight. Yes, you're right. Strictly business. And I'll be myself, but can I please get someone else's grace?"

Lori laughs. "Where are you going, anyway?"

"I haven't really worked that out yet." I switch on the coffee maker. The clock on it is exactly an hour and fifty-three minutes fast, so that makes it ten... no eleven, no.... somewhere around... shit, I slept the morning away.

"Well, go get some work done and I'll fill Nadine in to spare you from reliving the night again. Let me know how it goes."

"I will. Thanks Lor."

"You're welcome sweetie."

The aroma of French roast makes me feel more alive, and I prepare a workspace on my breakfast-bar counter. In an attempt to muffle the memory of last night's humiliation, I decide to ignore the list of ideas for my new assignment that is still in my bag and start fresh.

Foregoing my MacBook because my head cannot take the thought of a bright computer screen right now, I grab a pencil and a clean pad of paper from the kitchen drawer. Thankfully, the pencil is sharpened to a point, so my minor OCD is satisfied and I do not have to endure the pain of hearing the electric sharpener. I pour amaretto creamer into my coffee and get started.

First, I draw a long box and write a title on top: *"Come Here Often, a best-of series and exposé into the lives of six New Yorkers."* Under this heading, I begin to duplicate the chart I was going to show Anthony that listed the types of people I thought I should feature, then promptly erase it.

"You're not thinking about yesterday, remember?" I say aloud as I rub the lump on the back of my head. New day. New direction. Besides, upon further thought, it would probably be impossible, and definitely cliché, to find a New Yorker that fits each profile perfectly – the out of work actor, the aspiring model, the wall street executive, etc. So, what do I do? Approach any random person in a bar and ask if they 'come here often?'

Aside from their thoughts on the bar, what do we even talk about besides their job, interests, blah, blah, blah? How do I, ahem, dig deeper? I draw a shovel on my paper, which looks more like an arrow or an extremely swollen head of a penis – *not thinking about last night, not thinking about last night!* Then I take to doodling my name over and over again in bubble letters like I used to in middle school. A simpler, but apparently no more awkward, time in my life.

As I curse, this sudden onset of writer's block that seems to be becoming a habit, I am reminded of the list of desires that stumped me Friday morning. Then it hits me.

"*Come Here Often, a best-of series and exposé into the lives of six New Yorkers, with a personal focus on their pursuit of happiness.*" I give my readers the nightspot review they have come to trust, and, like the reality television shows they cannot get enough of, a voyeuristic glimpse into the lives of fellow New Yorkers out on a Saturday night. In the process of documenting their experiences, I conduct my own private study on happiness. If I can see life through other peoples' eyes, if only for one night, maybe it will lead me one step closer to finding the answers I am searching for.

Success in both aspects will hinge on my ability to capture the human element of the evening, by keeping my questions concise and allowing each person to tell their story through their own words and actions. It occurs to me that it should not be too difficult to get people to open up to me since, if I have learned one thing from all the horrible dates I have been on, it is that people love to talk about themselves. If I have learned another thing, it is that I tend to attract and be attracted to the most "interesting" people out there.

I easily think up six categories of nightspots, choose a place for the first one, then grab my phone and shake the butterflies off as I text Anthony the location and time to meet. Satisfied with my breakthrough, I spend the rest of the day catching up with my DVR and nursing my first hangover in I do not even remember how long. Essential to this recovery is devouring three pieces of a large greasy delivery pizza – I figure I am owed at least that many calories after not eating for two days – and taking a long princess shower, complete with sugar scrub and deep conditioning balm.

Before I know it, it is ten o'clock. I rifle through my closet and pick out a cute but comfortable outfit, then rush downstairs and out the door. When the misty night air hits me, so does the fact that I forgot to check the weather forecast. However, my brief, frizz-induced panic subsides with the realization that potential embarrassment over unruly hair is quite unsubstantiated, given the circumstances.

Taj is parked in his usual spot waiting for me. He has not been a minute late since we made our arrangement two years ago, after I hailed his cab to go on my first assignment for *The Socialite*. The magazine had not officially brought me on board yet, and was basing its decision on the article I would write about a punk rock club that had just opened in Staten Island. I was so nervous that I talked Taj's ear off the whole way there.

I did not think he was really listening, just nodding apathetically as cab drivers do, until we arrived at the bar and he asked if he could pick me up later to hear what I was going to write in my review. I told him he could, but he had to promise to drive me to and from every assignment if I got the job.

Only later did I find out that the magazine would pay me a stipend for a car service when I was on assignment. It all worked out though; cab fare is only a fraction of the amount, so I am able to tip Taj handsomely and have money leftover for three new pairs of shoes a month. Two if they are Jimmy Choos (on sale, of course).

Upon seeing me, Taj gets out and walks around the cab. He holds the back passenger door open with one hand, and a folded black umbrella with the other.

"If you have forgotten yours this evening, miss, you may borrow mine," he says in his thick accent.

"Thank you. Do you know you are the only man that never lets me down, Taj?" I reply as I duck inside.

"You should be talking to my wife... Where am I taking you tonight?"

"Buster's in the Seaport, please."

"We've been there before, yes?"

"Yes, my column's being changed a bit and I'm revisiting my favorite places for a few weeks. I'm also writing about the people I meet there."

"I see. Well, there are all kinds of people in this city for you to write about. Trust me on this one."

Taj recounts a few of the more eccentric passengers he has had as we make our way across the city, raindrops pattering on the roof of the cab and the radio playing faintly between his words. We are turning onto Fulton Street when a familiar Alicia Keys song catches my ear, yanking me from his story into a reluctant memory. I have not heard "Lesson Learned" since the last time my heart was broken. I played it over and over and over again the night I found Damon in our bed with the blonde with the butterfly tattoo.

Deep down, I knew the asshole was cheating from the beginning. But seeing it – her body rocking rhythmically on top of his, his hand stroking her hip, the wet spot on the gray sateen sheets – was something completely different. Loving the exceptionally undeserving, exceptionally fast and exceptionally hard, used to be a weakness of mine. A remote part of me aches along with Alicia, but her lyrics also serve as a reminder, literally and figuratively, that falling down is a prerequisite for getting back up. I just hope to maintain my balance this evening.

*****

I do not see Anthony out front so I head into Buster's, a small neighborhood place adorned with Lou "Buster" Gehrig baseball paraphernalia. With cozy booths, friendly bartenders, and mouth-watering fried food, it is the best spot in town, in my opinion, to catch a Yankees game. I still do not see him, so I grab a seat at the bar and order a club soda with lime.

It is early and the crowd is scarce, so I split my attention between the plasma TV screen in the center of the bar, and my BlackBerry, where I keep notes about the memories this place has brought back. It is the bottom of the eighth when a deep, sexy voice sidles up beside me.

"A sports bar, huh? I didn't peg you as a beer and peanuts kind of girl."

"Well there's a lot you don't know about me," I respond, reaching for a handful of the salty snacks from the wooden bowl on the bar. "For instance, that I can name the Yankee starting lineup alphabetically in less than six seconds. Adams, Almonte, Cano, Granderson, Murphy, Nunez, Reynolds, Ryan, Soriano, Warren. Or by batting average." Anthony laughs and the butterflies that had resurfaced start to fly away.

"No, it's okay. I get it. You like the Yankees."

"Yeah, but the games are so long I have to do something to keep myself occupied. Plus," I add quickly, "I thought it best to keep tonight as low key as possible, being our first assignment and all."

"Probably a good idea. I was disappointed that I didn't get to drop your name to cut a bunch of people in line tonight, though. How's your head feeling, anyway?" He reaches out to touch the almost disappeared bump, and I shiver not from pain, but from the novelty of a man's touch.

"Oh it's fine, really, and it's the last time I'll say it, but I'm very sorry about last night. I hadn't eaten anything all day and…"

He holds up his hands. "Forgotten."

"Cool, I appreciate that. Lisa," I call the bartender over, "can I get my friend a…?"

"Cranberry juice please. With a lemon."

"Sure you don't want a beer or something? I'm drinking club soda, but just because we're working doesn't mean…"

Cranberry's fine, thank you."

"Cranberry it is. So, where's your camera?"

"Right here." He stands up to grab a small compact out of his back pocket, and again the delayed reaction hits me of how fine he is, especially in just a button-up and jeans. "I didn't want to carry my big SLR around with me, and you know, attract a lot of attention, but don't worry, I can photograph just as well with this one."

I think it impossible for him not to attract a lot of attention. "Fine with me. You want to hear a few of my ideas before we get started?"

"Sure." And a crooked smile? God, he couldn't be any more perfect. *Focus, Athena.*

I reiterate the mission of our assignment and the format of my column, and tell him about the different categories of nightspots I have chosen. "I tried to make the list as diverse as possible in order to feature people from all walks of life. I'm not exactly sure what types of questions I'll ask, but my goal is to keep the conversation open and let our subjects do most of the talking. What do you think?"

"Like I said before, you're the writer. I'm just here to illustrate your words. So, yes, I'm down for whatever you have in mind."

"Alright, but don't hesitate to get involved, okay? This is a work in progress."

"Got ya. How are you going to pick our first victim?"

"Watch and learn."

I scan the room again, which has filled up with the typical Buster's crowd. Groups of co-ed friends huddle around tables, laughing and cheering at the baseball game, and the dartboards light up as young couples compete against each other and take turns picking music on the digital jukebox.

"That guy. There. Refilling a pitcher. Probably in his mid-twenties, wearing a white, long sleeve polo, and khaki cargo shorts. He's completely normal looking to me, which means there's the potential for some serious skeletons in his closet. Let's go." Anthony can barely catch up as I head to the end of the bar to introduce myself.

"Hey, I'm Athena Wallace from *The Manhattan Socialite*. I'm writing about Buster's tonight, and interviewing people about their experiences."

"Oh yeah? I think my sister reads your magazine. Always wants to know what's hot. Thinks she's like the Kim Kardashian of Brooklyn or something. Built more like Reggie Bush though. I'm Vince. Nice to meet you." He shakes my hand and I introduce my photographer.

"Do you come here often, Vince?" I ask, wincing internally at my use of such a tired phrase.

"My friends and I, we come here at least once a week. Love the place. I'm kind of on a date with someone though, and introducing her to all my boys, so I can't be gone too long or I'm afraid they'll scare her away. You're more than welcome to join us for a beer."

"We'd love to, thank you," I reply. Even though I feel sorry for this poor girl already, I cannot help being tempted by the impending storyline.

Vince motions to the bartender for two more frosted mugs, then we follow him to a corner table. Instead of the awkward scene I am expecting, we find this tiny little blonde thing arm-wrestling a big-boned Italian kid. His friends stare at her in awe as she slams his hand down with authority.

"Damn, you're a grown ass man, son, and she just killed you!" one of the guys taunts. "You're never hearing the end of this!" another guy says.

The girl is smiling confidently from ear to ear. "I told you guys I'm freakishly strong."

"Looks like she's a keeper," I whisper to Vince. He sets the pitcher down and puts his arm around his soon-to-be girlfriend.

"Guys, this is Athena, and Anthony. They work for that magazine that reviews places in the city, and I told them it was cool if they hung out with us for awhile." We are introduced to Rob, Tommy, Rico (the sore loser), and Theresa.

"She only beat me because I bench pressed my cousin this morning and pulled something."

"Yeah, right, man," Anthony says, slapping him on the back.

"Is that a challenge?" Theresa raises an eyebrow.

"No way, not after witnessing what happened to your last opponent." Rob and Tommy point and laugh at Rico again, and Vince beaming with pride, turns to me.

"So, what kind of questions do you want to ask us?"

"Well, first of all, what is it about Buster's that keeps you guys coming back?"

"We always come here to watch the Yankees. Beats the small-ass, old-school TV Rico's aunt gave us when we moved into our apartment. Thing's about forty years old probably, but hey, it was free. Every once in a while the antenna picks up Spanish-speaking porn too. Can't understand a word they're saying but who gives a shit, right? It's pretty awesome.

"Anyway, they also have the best hot wings outside of Buffalo and the only jukebox in town that has the entire *Escape* album from Journey. You know, the one that has "Don't Stop Believin'"? Not sure if you're familiar with it, but there's actually a lot of other good songs on that record. Plus, Rob is obsessed with the female bartenders here. Saturday is Lisa's shift so it's guaranteed that he's gonna take two hours getting ready, and when he finally emerges from the bathroom, it smells like he poured an entire bottle of 'CK One' all over himself."

"Shut the fuck up, Vince, I don't want them printing that shit." Rob punches his shoulder hard enough that Vince stumbles backward, and is shot a threatening 'don't blow it in front of my new girl' look.

"I won't, I swear." I type into my BlackBerry. "So... big TVs, hot wings, good music, professional bar staff... got it. Where you guys from anyway?" I take a sip of the beer Vince poured me and wish I hadn't. Not ready to get back on the horse yet.

Rico answers. "Me and the guys grew up together in the same neighborhood in Brooklyn... we live just over the bridge from here. We're all mechanics, and recently opened up a shop together called 4Brooklyn Mechanics," he holds up four fingers as he says it, to illustrate the spelling. "Kind of a cheesy name, I know. We're working on it, but business's been pretty good and we can't complain. Living the dream I guess... you two up for some darts? We can play teams," he does a head count while bending down to put quarters into a nearby machine and adds, "but shit, that's an odd number."

"It's cool; I have to take this anyway." Anthony looks down at the illuminated phone he has pulled from his shirt pocket, then disappears into the crowd to, I assume, step outside to take the call in private. The call from a girl? Girlfriend? Or one of many girlfriends? I mean, a guy that hot does not just date one person, or does he? Is he so gorgeous and artistic and mysterious that he is exclusively seeing a model? An Eastern European one with an exotic accent that did not accidentally hit him in the balls on their first date, err meeting, that can eat whatever she wants and still have a perfect body that half-nakedly graced the cover of last month's *Victoria's Secret* catalogue? Or, holy shit. What if she is not just his supermodel girlfriend with an overactive metabolism, but his supermodel fiancée?

The sound of the bulls-eye victory song and ensuing high fives snap me back to reality. *What the hell was that, Athena?* I reign in my internal freak-out and take the plastic darts from Tommy, whom I guess has recruited me to be on his team.

"You're up, sister. Fifteens are closed so try not to shoot those."

"Yeah, sure, okay," I stumble over my words, and toss the darts negligently at the board. Three straight zonk sounds, then I go retrieve them and place them in Vince's outstretched hands.

"Damn, you suck! Better stick to your day job, Barbara Walters," he says. Theresa giggles behind him, and, ignoring his flawed metaphor, I give him a sly smile before he shoots a double eighteen. I think it best to get back to business, if only to distract my mind from its illogical tangent.

"So, what other bars do you like to go to? Or is this your only spot?" I ask Tommy.

"Umm, it's usually Buster's for most of the night, and like Vince said before, if the Yanks are playing, but after Rob's fifth drink he'll beg Lisa for a date, she'll say no for the fiftieth time, then we'll all feel awkward and hit up another place or two before getting some grub and heading home. Which should be anytime now. What's this, number three?" Tommy playfully tips Rob's beer as he is taking a sip, causing foam to drip down his chin.

"I'm going to fucking kill you, Tommy. In your sleep. With your wrench."

"Don't get your panties in a bunch. You know it's true." Tommy turns away from his red-faced friend and toward me. "What about you? Why are you at this hole in the wall when you can get into the hottest clubs in the city? And more importantly, can you get *us* into the hottest clubs in the city? I heard the VIP room at Deluxx has girls dancing in feather thongs with tropical birds in cages hanging from the ceiling... I'm just sayin'."

Anthony rejoins the group and raises his eyebrows at me. "Wow, well I don't know about all that, but we were just catching the end of the game and doing a little research for my column. Actually, I do have a few more questions, do you mind if we tag along with you guys tonight?"

The dart game has temporarily come to a halt, and I now have the whole group's attention. After a few seconds of sideways glances at each other, Rico replies, "Um, Athena, no offense or anything, but if your name's on the guest list of places that have bird dancers and shit, why would you want to hang with guys like us?"

Sensing his friend may have misspoken, Vince interjects with, "And our beautiful, classy lady friend here." Satisfied with his save, and rewarded with a shy smile, he continues, "I thought you were doing research about Buster's anyway."

"Well, yes, we're doing an article on the appeal of Buster's, but it's more than that. It's also a story about a New Yorker--a group of New Yorkers--who I meet here." As I say this, I look them each in the eye, one by one, then continue, "I'll share a little bit about them, like how they spend a night out in the city, and Anthony will take photos to go along with the story.

"Starting here, now. So think about it guys. You could be featured in *The Socialite* next week, just for letting us hang with you. What do you think?" I purposely direct my question at Vince, who has already said yes to me once tonight, nominating him as the official spokesperson for his friends. He shrugs, attempting to look unimpressed, but the excitement in his eyes of potentially becoming a local celebrity for a week gives him away.

"Okay, sure. Sounds fun, and might be good for business. Right guys? You will mention our shop?"

"Absolutely," I reply.

The others nod in agreement, and I catch Theresa checking her makeup in the plexi-glass divider next to our table. I breathe a sigh of relief that the last half hour has not been spent in vain, and make a mental note to reveal my intent up front next time, as not to risk winding up with an unwilling protagonist at the end of the night.

"Great! Well, why don't we start by taking some photos of you finishing your dart game? Sign these," I pull five releases and a pen out of my purse, "and make sure to print your full name, legibly, with your contact info and date of birth. I'll grab us more beer."

The guys mockingly lick their hands and fix each others hair, and as I reach for the empty pitcher, Anthony's face leans into mine.

He covertly whispers, "Nicely done. That was easier than I thought it would be. It feels very 007, and I am thrilled that in this moment we are partners in crime."

"I can be very convincing," I whisper back.

Four dart games, two pitchers, five impromptu getting-to-know-you conversations, and a dozen or so ridiculously raunchy jokes later, I glimpse Rob leaning over the beer taps and talking to Lisa, who has a polite but uncomfortable look about her. He bends a little too far in, and I see her jump backward and rush to grab a rag as draft beer spurts all over her shirt and onto the rubber mat beneath her feet.

"Guys," I gesture toward the bar, "I think it's time to go."

"Ah shit, well that's about right." Rico checks his watch and makes a circular motion above his head. "Gather the troops."

I pinch my straw and slurp up the bottom of my third club soda – which I have not been given a hard time about due to, I believe, it's resemblance of a vodka tonic – and turn to Vince.

"What's up next?"

"I'm thinking Pier 52 for one more before heading home." He looks from side to side to see if Theresa has returned from the ladies room before whispering to me, "They have karaoke there tonight, and I want to sing for her."

Touched and a little shocked by his confession, I say, "Sounds good. Let me go freshen up and I'll tell her we're meeting outside."

I find Theresa applying a thick layer of pink lip gloss in the cracked, full-length bathroom mirror, and go to the oval one above the dripping faucet to dust on some powder. I usually do not wear foundation, but the humidity tonight is on some serious shit. I relay the plan to her, omitting of course the potential serenade, and in an instant she is by my side and we are girlfriends. Her expression is a combination of deep concern and stifled giddiness, and I find myself a bit jealous that the wrinkles in her furrowed brow have not yet made a permanent impression on her young – twenty-two year old – skin.

"Athena, I really like him, like more than I've ever liked anyone before. He's so cute and kind and funny, and really driven, you know? You seem like you might have experience with this stuff. How do I show him I'm interested without embarrassing myself in front of his friends?"

I find it mildly humorous that she takes my age for experience – well, positive experience anyway. I snap my compact closed and turn to meet her blue-gray eyes in her reflection.

"Sweetie, I don't think you have anything to worry about. Really. I get the feeling he likes you too, a lot. He took you here to meet his friends, right? To show you off! A guy would never bring a girl around his boys if he didn't think she was amazing, *and* if he didn't plan on her being around for awhile." Her face relaxes a little and a small smile creeps across her cotton candy lips.

"And did you see those guys out there? You'd have to put a concerted effort into embarrassing yourself in front of those fools." She giggles as I grab her hand and move towards the door. "Come on, they're waiting on us." But Theresa's feet remain planted on the ground and seriousness washes over her.

"Promise me you won't write anything about this?"

"I swear." The cross I make over my heart seems to appease her, and we head outside where the guys are huddled under the entrance awning, arms around one another, posing for Anthony.

The walk to Pier 52 is short but wet. The boys run ahead of us through the downpour, and I share the small umbrella Taj lent me with Theresa. Although it does an adequate job of saving my hair, the harbor winds drench my exposed left side and dishevel my outfit. We duck into the warm, dry space and when I am finally done getting my scarf, blouse, and hoop earrings back into place, I look up to take in the atmosphere before me. Never having stepped foot in this place before, I am pleasantly surprised to see that it is much nicer on the inside than the ramshackle wooden exterior conveys.

A dive bar, definitely, but there is something charming about the wood paneling and vintage liquor decor. Neon beer signs and strands of twinkling Christmas lights give the room a dusky glow, and I feel like I am in an old friend's basement. If I was not still under the wrath of yesterday's calamity, a snifter of cognac might make me all warm and toasty here.

Vince is chatting up the bartender, a salt and pepper haired man sporting a well-trimmed mustache, whom I can tell just by looking at mixes a fantastic cocktail. Rico, Tommy and Rob are trying to convince Theresa to chug one of the four Irish car bombs that already sit in front of them, while Anthony leans against the bar, gazing at his camera screen. Vince pats the empty bar stool next to him, and I hop up and take a seat.

"Another vodka tonic?"

I hold my hand up. "I'm good, thanks."

"Well, will you help me pick out a song then?" He slides a red three-ring binder over to me that has "song choices" scribbled on the cover in black marker. I flip through the sticky pages, find what I am looking for, and slide it back to him.

"Do you," I say.

He looks down and grins slightly. "I'm a little nervous, I've never sung in front of anyone before. Bet the guys'll never let me live this one down."

"It will so be worth it." I squeeze his sweaty hand and signal to the bartender for one shot of Patron. Vince gives me a quick "Cheers" before drinking the tequila, then makes his way to the preoccupied brunette standing behind the small deejay booth. She takes the open binder from him and points to the makeshift stage without breaking concentration from her cell phone. He slowly walks to the microphone stand in the center of the room, as his face takes on a red, blue, then green glow from the spinning disco light above.

Rob hits his two friends' arms, and cocks his head toward the fourth member of the group. Their jaws drop simultaneously. As the music explodes loudly from the ancient speakers, the six other bar patrons casually and amusingly direct their attention to the young man. Clutching the mic with grease-stained fingers, Vince runs his other hand through his slick hair before timidly reciting the first verse of Journey's "Open Arms."

Disregarding the lyrics that race across the glowing monitor, he searches for Theresa's eyes. When he finds them, she has to steady herself by leaning back onto the stool behind her. His confidence builds with every note, the tip of his tongue caressing each syllable as if he is composing the song in this exact moment, for her. Upon reaching the chorus, Vince goes for it. With more richness and conviction than I could have ever imagined. This Brooklyn boy's got soul.

The boys burst into loud applause, and we can hardly hear as he finishes the refrain. I look around for Anthony to see what he thinks of the scene, but do not find him anywhere. I smother the voice in my head that is asking if perhaps he has stepped outside to take another phone call from a supermodel.

Meanwhile, Vince is met with shoulder grabs and "no fucking way bro's," but pushes past his posse toward Theresa.

"Did you like it?"

She responds with a giant hug and a peck on the cheek. She starts to whisper something in Vince's ear when a wobbly Rico spins him around. "What the hell was that, man? I've never even heard you hum!"

"If you had a mullet I might've mistaken you for Steve Perry. I'm not kidding, that shit gave me the chills," Tommy says.

"Fucking awesome," adds Rob.

"Thanks, guys," Vince replies modestly. "I gotta give Theresa credit. She's the whole reason I got up the courage to go up there. Never thought I'd sing in front of anyone, let alone a bunch of people."

Theresa wraps her fingers around his damp polo and pulls him close, her lips moving softly in his ear.

"Well, it's been real, but I've got to get Theresa on the train before it gets too late." He helps her into her jacket, his movements dripping with a newfound swagger, and waves goodbye to me. "Pleasure to meet you, Athena. Thanks for everything tonight. Hope your article comes out good."

"Thank you for letting me tag along." I notice Theresa hesitate as he opens the door for her, and I rush over to hand her my umbrella. "Keep it. You deserve to have good hair tonight." She takes it with appreciation, locks her arm around Vince's elbow, and they are off into the misty night to write their own ending.

With plenty of time before last call, and anxious to get home and into some dry pajamas, I decide I have everything I need. I say my goodbyes, convincing the guys I do not need to be accompanied to my cab – such unexpected gentlemen! – and manage to slip away without taking the murky, foul smelling shot Tommy insists I must have to commemorate the evening. I make it three-quarters of the way to the door before I see the back of my photographer's head leaving the restroom.

"Anthony! There you are," I remark offhandedly. "Did you catch the performance?"

"I did. Should make for a pretty good story, huh?"

"Definitely. Do you think you got enough pictures? I was just heading out."

"Yes. Let me grab my coat and I'll walk you," he replies.

Taj is already parked where he left me in front of Buster's as Anthony and I uneventfully part ways.

"Need a lift?" I ask. *Please say yes...*

"No thanks, I'm all set." *Damn.* I am disappointed, but too stuck in my own head, already piecing together my article, to overanalyze anything right now. I unwrap the soaked scarf from my hair and plop down.

"Hi Taj, I'm so glad you're here already. I thought I might have to call you."

"Slow night," he responds, as he shifts into drive.

I pull out my BlackBerry and type a few ideas while they are fresh in my head, fighting the sleep that the slish-slosh of the windshield wipers is lulling me into. We arrive at my building and just as I am getting out, I remember something.

"Oh Taj, I'm sorry, I gave your umbrella to a friend. I owe you one."

His gentle eyes crease. "People leave them in here all the time. You don't owe me anything Athena, except of course your fare."

*****

Monday morning comes so much sooner than I am ready for it too. After arriving at the office, I delete all the emails in my spam folder, draw hearts in my coffee with the stirrer, and play a pickup game of trashcan basketball with the three crumpled up pages from my quote-a-day calendar. I finally decide it is time to stop procrastinating and pull the tortoise shell Ray Bans from my top desk drawer. They are neither prescription nor at all optically necessary, but when I wear them I feel so much smarter and a little sexier too. The thought crosses my mind that I should bring these on my next date, whenever that will be.

The first task of the day is to email the notes from my BlackBerry to myself so I can open them on my desktop, cut and paste them into my publishing software, then later sync the document to my laptop. It is a reoccurring pain in the ass. I know I should get an iPhone to streamline the process, but am entirely too clumsy with a touch screen keyboard.

I also refuse to haul an ugly laptop bag to and from work, and prefer a bigger monitor to flip between the Internet, email, my blog, and column. So, essentially, I am stuck in a digital hell of my own creation. I am about to press 'send' when the screen flashes a text from Nadine.

"Sooo …. Saturday night?!?!? Details pleeeease!!!"

I sigh and realize I forgot to update the girls yesterday as promised. Before I can respond, it lights up again. This time Lori, who I now see has been copied in on the message.

"Everyone's scrotum intact I hope?"

I giggle to myself, that's such an awful word! I really do have to get started, though, so I type,

"NOTHING happened, all business. Sorry to disappoint. Working on column, catch up with you ladies later. xoxo"

I finish emailing and see that Nadine has added *"Bore"* to our message chain before flipping my phone over and getting to work.

A knock at the door causes me to jump in my seat, and I look up to see Mark batting his big hazel eyes at me. I bite on the stem of my glasses and squint at him. His face has an unusual color about it.

"I'm sorry to startle you honey, I just wanted to see if you'd like to grab lunch?"

I flip my phone back over and see that it is already noon. Time flies when I am writing.

"Nah, I'm kind of in the zone here, but if you go downstairs could you pick me up a cup of minestrone with those little crackers? Oooh, and an unsweetened iced tea. I'd love you forever. Are you wearing bronzer?"

"Just a little something I'm trying. And of course I will. First, you have to tell me all about your weekend. Did you go out with *him*?" He leans in to emphasize the last word, and I notice that he is also experimenting with mascara.

"Yes, *Anthony* and I worked together and that is all. It... the evening... the assignment," I say, stumbling over my words, "went better than expected."

"Mm, hmm. I bet it did."

I lower my voice and point in his tan face. "Listen, I wish I had more to tell you but I don't. Seriously, what's up with this?" I run my finger down his nose and show him the brown smudge.

"These fluorescent's make me look sad. Not enough natural light. I'm just trying to spruce the place up a bit," he says, fluffing a pretend bob cut.

"Mark, I hate to break it to you, but you're a boy. And bald! That shade doesn't even look natural on you. Buuut you did just give me an idea." I grab the purple post-its and scribble a note to myself.

He frowns at me and crosses his arms. "I'm not sure I like your tone. According to the pleasant lady at the makeup counter, this shade, Café Au Lait, is perfect for my alabaster complexion. It is also very hot among European businessmen.

And for the record, I cut it short. My hair, that is." He storms out in overdramatic fashion, flipping his imaginary coiffure behind his shoulder, and two seconds later reappears in the doorway. "I'll be right back with your soup."

While it is on my mind, I pick up the phone and dial Brian's extension.

"Hello Athena, how did the first week of your best-of series go? Find someone interesting to write about?" he asks.

"It went really well. I should have it off to you by mid-week. I was just thinking, are you set on having the person I interview be a customer of the establishment? Or is it okay with you if I consider a staff member if the opportunity presents itself?"

"If it sells magazines, you could write about a fruit fly. As long as you stick to the theme we discussed, I'm all right with leaving the details up to you."

"Great, thanks Brian. I'll touch base in a few days." That takes care of the plan for week two.

The glasses go back on to review the morning's efforts. The review portion of my column is done, followed by an outline of the story of his Vince and his friends, and an ending to bring it all together:

Just like the atmosphere inside of Buster's sports bar, the relationship between these four friends from Brooklyn is comfortable and unpretentious, with an irresistible feeling of hometown charm. Whether sharing a cold beer or a hot date, both are there... with Open Arms.

Pleased with what I have so far, I go back to fill in the details of their story. As I consider the events of Saturday night, I cannot help feeling pretty smug about my role in fanning the flames of young borough love. So sweet, so simple. Why can't I accomplish that in my own life? It is a rhetorical question, since I already know why. It is because I overcomplicate *everything.*

If you really think about it, romance is not that complex of a thing. In its purest form, it involves two people, chemistry, and the fortitude to act on it with enthusiasm and mutual respect. What it definitely does *not* involve is having a stroke over who is on the other end of a phone call to a potential suitor, or more precisely, a co-worker. It should not be that hard or stressful. So... I am done with the Anthony thing. Well, I will give it my best effort to be done with it. *Easy, breezy Athena for the next five weeks, as far as Anthony is concerned.* That is the goal. Besides, I am getting too old for this shit. Now where was I?

My soup arrives just in time. Time for a lunch break. I prepare to play a little game of Real Bag/Fake Bag on eBay, the science behind which has taken years of dedicated research to master, when something else catches my eye. There it is, loitering unapologetically in the bottom right corner of the tool bar. *My Desires.*

Damn, I cannot escape myself today. I click open the document, highlight the five items on it and hit 'delete.' Good riddance, Gucci bag. Sure, I *could* technically afford a new one of you before you are available via online auction, but that would deprive me of the didn't-pay-retail rush, my particular brand of crack, and would require a serious rebalancing of the Excel sheet budget for this month, something I promised myself I would never do.

My fingers tap along the side of the keyboard in anticipation of some sort of epiphany. What have I learned from my first best-of assignment slash social experiment? What, if any, are the potential implications for my own search for happiness? Those are big questions that I am not sure how to answer yet. I will have to start by asking the smaller ones.

Like... what desires are shared by Vince, Rob, Tommy, and Rico?

Well, based solely on my observations, interviews, and small talk over the course of a few hours: a successful business of their own; financial security; to be rewarded for a hard day at work with laughter, alcohol, and the company of good friends; and dating the attractive girl-next-door type – I will assume they are not at the marriage/kids stage yet. They are also all into muscle cars and hook ups, but for my purposes, I will classify these things as *wants*.

This raises another question concerning the difference between wants and desires. In this context, I would define a want as a momentary, static inclination, like a wish, whereas a desire, I believe, involves having a deeper commitment to something. With this, when I attempted to write my desire list last week, I was hung up on the difference between desires and goals. Upon further thought, it seems that the two are related but not interchangeable, since a desire requires a strong emotional attachment, but a goal does not. I sense a minor revelation in this distinction, but I do not know what to do with it.

So, the next logical question then, becomes whether achieving these desires leads Vince and his friends to be fulfilled, and not just at a superficial level. I sip the room temperature soup as I ponder this one. *Hmmm. I think the answer is yes ...?* They seemed like well-adjusted, happy people, yet it would not be fair to pigeonhole them as 'simple' either. I am not even sure how to quantify happiness. Vince was clearly proud, excited, happy, whatever you want to call it, about achieving his desire (a relationship with Theresa), but how does that relate to his overall state of mind? Being in love can be extraordinary, but it certainly is not all that is required for a happy life.

To take it one step further, though, say the stars just happen to align and every single one of your desires is fulfilled, whether you are able to name them all or not. Is that true happiness? Can the equation really be that linear? Does $x + y$ always $= z$? And if it does, if all this is true, regardless of its probability, how does this help me discover what I genuinely desire so I can begin my journey toward leading a happier, more fulfilled life?

At this point, I discouragingly have more questions than answers. I am afraid this exhausting mental exercise has been in vain, and a giant waste of time. Don't Eastern philosophers spend their entire lives grappling with, not even answering these type of questions? There are thousands of books addressing the subject of happiness, and Athena Wallace thinks she can solve it all over a cup of minestrone. A part of me knows I am overcomplicating again, but I am done with this for now. I close the still empty page and get back to the much simpler task of writing my column.

*****

It's 4:02 on Wednesday before I hear from Anthony. He shows up in my office with a disk of photos from our first assignment together.

"So... how's the article coming?" he asks.

"It's done, thank you. Pretty much wrote itself. All that's left is to choose a couple photos. I'm hoping you have one of Vince on stage?"

"Yeah, there's actually a great one of him singing with Theresa in the background. Her expression is priceless." He tosses the plastic case to me. "Sorry it took so long to get this to you, I'm juggling a few projects right now. Do you need anything else from me?"

I can think of a few things, none of which involve work, or clothes. *Easy breezy, Athena*, I remind myself. *Easy breezy.*

"No, I think I'm good. Aren't you interested in where our next adventure will be?" *Oh God.* The crooked smile makes an appearance again. Doesn't it know that it is the middle of the week and it is not invited into my office? Doesn't it know that I have taken a vow of celibacy from caring? "I hope you're okay with this... " I hand him the Mark-inspired post-it.

"Wild Horses. Never heard of it," Anthony replies. He shrugs and sticks his incredibly juicy bottom lip out. It is begging to be bit.

"Welllll, it falls under my best-of category for a gay bar. There are two Broadway-worthy drag shows a night. I'm hoping we can catch the matinee – they call it the 'man'inée'– so I can rub elbows with a member of the cast. If all goes well, shadow her/him for the night."

Anthony folds the note and puts it into the pocket of his perfectly tailored charcoal slim-fits. "I have no problem with that. My pops raised me to pass no judgments."

Your pops raised you to be fine. "Great, the show starts at six. I'm guessing you don't care if we make it in time for happy hour? The grapefruit mar-gay-rita's are to die for."

"Six sounds good. See you then." He hesitates before leaving. "If you don't mind, send me your article. I want an exclusive first-look."

Oh, I'll give you something to look at.

"Will do. See you this weekend."

Suffice to say, I am relieved to see him go. I pop in the CD-rom and can instantly confirm that Brian was not wrong about this man's talent. Vince's anticipation, Theresa's shock and awe, Tommy's kind eyes, Rob and Rico's blue-collar charm. It is all there in the photographs, even emotions that I was not cognizant of at the time. It is difficult, but I choose one landscape of Buster's interior and two of the Brooklynites, then email everything off to the editing department, Brian, and Anthony. Not ten minutes later there is a reply in my inbox:

"Re: Come Here Often, Week 1," from my overzealous boss.

Thank you for sharing this ahead of deadline. Fantastic work Athena and Anthony! Exactly what I had in mind. Keep it up. Can't wait to read next week's.

A compliment from Brian is... rare, to say the least, so I chalk up my initial efforts on this project to success, more professional than personal that is. As the desktop powers down, my thoughts turn to hope that a) I still have that bottle of Riesling in the fridge and b) someone will catch an ass whippin' on tonight's DVR'd episode of *The Real Housewives of Atlanta*.

Happiness At a Holocaust Museum?

CHAPTER 4

"Why so early this week, miss?" Taj asks as he opens the taxi door.

"Seeing a show at Wild Horses in the East Village," I reply, as I tuck the tulle of my plum, floor length ballerina skirt between my legs. I have been drooling over an excuse to finally wear this, an impulsive buy at my favorite off-the-runway boutique that's pricey, although deeply discounted, was still in no way, *ever*, justifiable.

Tonight's venue seems as good a place as any to wear it. Plus it goes well with my nude, sky-high patent leather heels, which, if I do say so myself, makes my ass look divine. Thankfully, my photographer is well over six-feet tall, so he will still have a good four to five inches on me tonight (although his eight or nine, I'm guessing, *in me* would be ideal). *Easy, Athena...* Nevertheless, we will not look awkward standing together if someone were to just so happen to mistake us for a couple.

"Do you mind being on call tonight?" I ask Taj. "I'm not sure what the evening has in store."

"It is no problem. The East Village you say."

I arrive a few minutes after six, and see that Anthony is waiting on a cheetah-print barstool. His foot taps the bottom of the bar, which is made entirely of an aquarium filled with light turquoise water and saltwater fish. Hovering near his toe is a clown fish, and near his chest, the bartender, dressed as Marilyn Monroe. She is giggling at something he has said, and lightly fingering his tweed blazer.

Beyoncé's "If I Were A Boy" provides the soundtrack to the scene, while the music video plays on hundreds of mini TVs that make up the dance floor, already packed with twirling bodies. The highlight of the room is the elaborate catwalk, which wraps around the stage above the dance floor and extends on both sides up to the second level. Upstairs it forms a big loop around the room, about thirty feet in the air, where a dozen stripper poles shimmer under the reflection of a giant hot pink disco ball. Calling this place 'flamboyant' would be an understatement.

Marilyn seems taken aback as I pull up a seat shaped like the bottom half of a zebra. Anthony seems relieved. Her expression quickly changes as she studies my face.

"Athena? Athena Wallace? Is that you, girl?"

"It's me." She wraps her enormous biceps around me.

"I recognize you from your picture in *The Socialite*! You are more beautiful in person and just like royalty around here. After you wrote that rave review on us last year, we were bursting at the seams with queens! Have been ever since! Are you back to write a follow-up?" She pulls back from our embrace, squeezing my arms intensely.

"Something like that. You'll be happy to hear I'm naming you guys... um girls... I mean, you all, best gay bar in the city. In a new series for my column called *Come Here Often*."

Marilyn clasps her hands in delight. "Oooooh that's such great news! I can't wait to tell the boys. Anything you want tonight, on the house." She waves at the extensive selection of booze.

I eye Anthony's cranberry juice, which has been served in a hurricane glass complete with a tiny umbrella and a Carmen Miranda-worthy fruit kebab on a penis-shaped cocktail stirrer.

"I'll take one of those. With Grey Goose please." Marilyn turns away to fix my drink, and I carefully reach down into my bag to get my phone.

"I'm sorry I'm late. Seems like Marilyn took a liking to you," I say to Anthony.

"I take the attention as a compliment," he replies, as he stretches over me to grab a napkin to wipe his nose. I notice that his eyes are puffy. "Hey, are you sick?"

"I'm okay, just a little cold, I think. What is that thing, anyway, some sort of primitive typewriting device?" he asks, nodding towards my Blackberry. He sounds congested, which makes his already deep voice two octaves lower. *Damn if he doesn't make sick look sexy.*

"Funny stuff coming from the man with the fruit cock-tail. You gonna eat that?"

"No, please, take it," he says, dipping the phallic stirrer into my drink as Marilyn sets it in front of me.

The lights flash on and off twice to signal the start of the show. We turn our attention to the stage, to an exquisitely dressed drag queen sporting a mile high bouffant.

"Good evening ladies and ladies, welcome to Wild Horses! Thank you so much for joining us. I'll be your hostess, the modern-day Marie Antoinette. It's the Queen of Queens y'all, best known for my gay rights activism and the phrase, let them eat cock!"

I turn to gauge Anthony's reaction, but see that he has left his seat to take some photos. "We have four incredible divas taking the stage tonight, the first two during our man'inée, when we say the early bird gets the worm." She rolls her body, rubbing herself up and down with white-gloved hands as she emphasizes the word 'worm.' "Or at least we hope so, right girls?"

"That's right, Marie!" someone in the crowd yells.

"The first act will be followed by a short intermission, and after the second act there will be a foam dance party. I promise you don't want to miss it, things tends to get awful wet around here! Then, at eleven, our late show begins. You are such a gorgeous crowd, I hope you will stay with us all evening. What do you say?" The music plays as our hostess belts out "Wiiiiild, wild horses, couldn't"– she extends the microphone to the audience who scream "drag!" – then she finishes with, "you away. You all are wonderful!

"Now, without further ado, allow me to introduce our opening act. She's an old friend of ours that I'm sure you'll recognize. I think I see her –" Marie puts her hands over her eyes as she scans the room. The spotlight flashes around until it finds its petite target, her arms draped around one of the poles upstairs. She's wearing a straight black wig, a bedazzled beret, and an elaborate can-can outfit that puts my skirt to shame. "Yes, there she is! I see London, I see... Francey!" The crowd goes wild.

"Thank you! Thank you, Queen Marie, and everyone for being here tonight!" Francey takes a drag from her long, skinny cigarette through an elegant metal holder. "I'd like to start the show with an old favorite of mine. This is dedicated to all the men I've loved and lost. Well, I guess they're the ones who've lost, now isn't that right ladies?" A surprisingly moving rendition of "My Funny Valentine" follows, and after an hour of classic musical numbers, she finishes with a show-stopping performance of "Lady Marmalade" that includes a sparkler bra, twelve gorgeous, shirtless men gyrating on the stripper poles, and feathers falling from the ceiling.

The lights go up, and Marilyn rushes over to see if I need a refill. "One's my limit tonight, but a club soda would be nice." She sticks the soda gun in my glass and pours the beverage over the alcohol infused ice.

"So, what'd you think of the first act?" she asks.

"Even better than the last time I was here. Is there a chance I could talk to Francey?"

"Sure, honey, she should be coming around to the bar in a few. I'll introduce you. Do you think your handsome friend would like a drink?"

"No, I think my *straight* friend is all set," I say with a smile.

"Point taken sweetie, but you better rub your scent all over that one before someone else in here tries to. Let me know if you need anything else." She pivots to serve one of the still shirtless dancers on my left, and I have to retrieve my phone to distract myself from his glistening pecs.

I type a few thoughts before Anthony joins me at the bar.

"That was incredible. I never knew a man could be so... nimble," he says, then points behind me to an enthusiastic Marilyn who's flagging us down the bar.

"Athena, Athena come over here," she shrieks. "There's someone I want you to meet!"

I tug Anthony's soft palm and get about halfway to where she is standing before realizing this is the first time we have had physical contact – intentionally and above the belt, that is. I shake it off, and drop his hand to greet the one and only Francey. If you could look past the trace of facial hair and Adam's apple, she is actually quite stunning up close.

"Hi, I'm Athena Wallace. Your show was spectacular! Francey, is it?"

"Thanks, baby," she says warmly, as she removes the mole over her lip and takes a sip of blush colored wine. "Yes, it's Francey. You know, like fancy with an 'r'? Francey the tranzey? Anywho, I hear we owe you quite a bit of gratitude around here." Her smile reveals a sizable gap between her two front teeth – a normally unfavorable feature that is striking on her.

"Me? Please. I just call it like it is, and this place is amazing. Would you mind if I asked you a few questions for my column? By the way, this is Anthony; he works for *The Manhattan*

Socialite as a photographer." Francey looks him up and down before extending her bony hand.

"It would be my pleasure. *And you.* I noticed you taking pictures during my act. If you ever want to do a private shoot, you just let Francey know."

My stomach drops and I feel a twinge of guilt for bringing his fine ass here, even though he seems to be taking it all in stride. I pose a few questions about the appeal of performing at Wild Horses before springing my ulterior motive on her. "So, what do you think? Could Anthony and I shadow you tonight?"

"That's fine with me, but I'm going to --" she's muted by the sound of Marie Antoinette introducing the next act.

"I'm sorry, you're going where?" I ask loudly. I still cannot discern Francey's answer and give her a puzzled look. "Shoes! The museum is about the history of shoes!" She yells over the roar of the crowd, as a six-foot J-Lo impersonator with padded booty shorts takes the stage.

I smile and nod, but on the inside I am jumping up and down for joy. *How is it possible that there is a shoe museum in Manhattan and I have never heard of it, let alone been there?* I tear open my bag in search of a release form, and after she fills it out, she mouths over a low octave cover of "Jenny from the Block" that she will meet us out front in twenty minutes.

Anthony takes a few more photos of the bar while I visit the cramped unisex bathroom to ensure my hair and makeup are in place, and call Taj. Then we stand outside to wait. And wait. And wait.

Leaning on the cab next to Anthony, I make a few attempts in spite of myself to strike up a casual conversation about the weather, the drag show, anything not related to work, but each time his reply is brief and followed by either a sneezing fit or the arrival of a text message. Finally, I give up and bury myself in my digital notepad. I am almost done outlining the entire first half of my article when a short, balding man with a gruffly voice comes up behind us.

"There you are. Sorry I took so long. I just about have to take a sandblaster to my face to get all that makeup off. You ready?" If it had not been for the empty space in the middle of his smile, I might not have recognized Francey. Her persona appears to have changed with her outfit, which now consists of a shapeless brown sport coat and black corduroy pants. We both stare at the little fellow in disbelief, before I curtail our rudeness.

"Francey, is that you? You look so different out of drag!"

"Yeah baby, I know. That's the point though, right? Is this our cab?"

"Yes, here." I open the door for her, now a him, and go around to the other side, raising my eyebrows at Anthony as he gets into the front seat.

"Taj, meet my co-worker Anthony, and this is Francey."

"Nice to meet you. Now what is the address to where we are going?" Taj asks.

"1109 Fifth Avenue please, on the corner of 92nd Street," Francey replies.

Funny, I have been to Carnegie Hill hundreds of times, but have never noticed a shoe museum there. Taj pulls out into traffic, and, without giving it another thought, I begin to interview the unlikely star of *Come Here Often*, week two, in more detail about his career.

Interestingly enough, I uncover that Columbia Law School was what attracted Francey to New York from the small, midwestern town where he was raised. An honor society scholar and glee club member, dressing in drag began as a hobby until, as fate would have it, his closeted ethics professor was in the audience during an amateur night performance at a local gay bar.

"Back in the eighties, the old boys club ran the legal community, and there was no such thing as a non-discrimination policy, especially for sexual orientation. I suppose it was an effort to secure tenure, because a week later I got a letter from the financial aid office notifying me that my scholarship was being pulled due to circumstances beyond their control. So, if I wanted to stay in school, I had to make a lot of money, fast."

Francey quickly made a name for himself in the "queer club circuit," as he calls it, and the day after passing the bar exam, was offered a staring role in the off-Broadway production of *La Cage aux Folles*. He traveled extensively throughout Europe with the show, but two years later a nasty fall from a high wire act left him with two broken legs, a shattered pelvis, and the premature ending to his professional acting career. The tragedy resulted in a multi-million dollar civil suit.

"But honey, if you think I'm convincing as a woman, you should see me in the courtroom."

After making a full recovery, Francey returned to the stage and his roots in the Manhattan club scene. He tells me that another passion of his is serving as a legal consultant, pro bono, for Tri-State Area LGBT groups, and describes a few of the human rights violation cases he has won on their behalf.

I consider probing into his personal life, but the cab is slowing, and we pull up alongside a tall cement structure. Francey is halfway out of the door and I am sliding over to get out on his side when he stops in his tracks. "A thought just occurred to me. I am very sorry, but I don't think they allow cameras in the exhibit."

Anthony turns in his seat to face me. I tell Francey to go on ahead, and that I will catch up with him in the museum.

"Why don't you go home? You're obviously not feeling well, and there's no sense of you being here without your camera," I tell Anthony.

"No, I'm not leaving you here by yourself."

"It's totally fine, I swear. Francey seems harmless. Besides, even if he's not, I'm pretty sure I could take him."

That gets a laugh out of him, but he is still reluctant to leave.

"Taj, please take Anthony home. I'll cover the fare when you come back to pick me up. I'll call you when I'm done."

He has another sneezing fit, and Taj hands him a tissue from the compartment in his door.

"Alright, I'll go," he acquiesces after blowing his nose. "But you're not covering my fare, and you will buzz me if you need anything, okay? My services are a phone call away."

Oh, if only that were true.

I agree to his terms, and start heading towards the front of the building. It is then that I notice the banner out front that is flapping in the wind. *Welcome to Opening Night of "The Life and Times of Holocaust Survivors."* When I had a hard time hearing Francey over the noise, he must have said Jews, not shoes! The museum is about the history of Jews! Disappointment over tonight's turn of events washes over me as I turn to watch the taillights of the cab disappear down Fifth Avenue.

*****

A table of smiling staff meets me at the museum entrance. I smile back politely and walk towards the gathering, but an elderly lady with a clipboard calls after me.

"Name please? Did you make an advance reservation?"

"Reservation? My name's Athena Wallace. My friend just came in a minute ago. He might have put me on the list. Francey."

She scrolls down her pad of paper. "Who? And you said your name is what? I don't see you on here. Tickets for tonight's private showing are one hundred dollars ma'am."

"Well I'm a reporter so I'm just gonna – " I flash my press pass and attempt to slide by, but she outstretches her palm with authority.

"One hundred dollars, ma'am. To benefit the museum."

"This keeps getting better and better," I grumble into my wallet.

I find Francey just past the string quartet, studying a dreary still life of a concentration camp.

"Hey Francey, sorry about that. I figured Anthony didn't need to stay. So what's this exhibit–"

Speaking in a soft voice. "Athena, I'd appreciate it if in here you would call me Francis."

"Francis?"

"Yes, my name. I hope you gave it to them at the door? It's spelled out on that paper you had me sign back at the club."

I shake my head. "Oh dear, you had to pay. I'll go straighten this out right now. Be right back." He kisses my cheek and disappears into the lobby.

Now standing alone, I am suddenly self-conscious about the contrast of my whimsical frock amidst the somber ambiance. Disregarding my self-imposed drink minimum, I pluck a glass of funny tasting sparkling wine – Manischewitz? – from a tray passing by, and peer into my purse to find the aforementioned release. I unfold the signature portion to confirm that, yes, in fact I am spending the evening with one "Francis Edelstein."

Admitting that I have to make the best of the situation for the sake of my column, I shift focus to the portrait before me entitled Prisoner number 119104. The description reads as follows:

Viktor Frankl was an Austrian psychiatrist, neurologist, and author, and the founder of logotherapy. In 1942, Frankl was sentenced to three years in a Nazi concentration camp alongside his parents and his wife. He was the sole survivor among them. While imprisoned, Frankl counseled inmates and helped them deal with the devastating emotional toll of camp life. His observations about grief and resiliency became the foundation for his bestselling book, released one year after his liberation, Man's Search for Meaning

(1946). Frankl's existentialist ideology can be summed up by the following passage from this book:

> "This uniqueness and singleness which distinguishes each individual and gives a meaning to his existence has a bearing on creative work as much as it does on human love. When the impossibility of replacing a person is realized, it allows the responsibility, which a man has for his existence and its continuance to appear in all its magnitude. A man who becomes conscious of the responsibility he bears toward a human being who affectionately waits for him, or to an unfinished work, will never be able to throw away his life. He knows the 'why' for his existence, and will be able to bear almost any 'how.'"

Enthralled, I read the passage a second time and denote "Viktor Frankl" and "logotherapy" in my BlackBerry notes. Preoccupied with dissecting the words I have just stumbled upon as they relate to the personal side of this assignment, I wander through the museum for a short time before Francis returns to my side in front of the hors d'oeuvres table. He has a hundred-dollar bill in hand.

"Here's your money, honey. So, what do you think of the exhibit? The Jews are such fascinating people, aren't we?"

"That you are," I say, before swallowing my first and last bite of kosher pâté. "How did you hear about this private showing, anyway? Are you a member of the museum?"

"I sit on the board of directors, have for years. An ex-boyfriend of mine from many, many moons ago is actually the curator here. When he found out I was back living in New York, he reached out to me and asked if I would consider becoming a board member. We always shared a love for history; that, and beekeeping."

"Beekeeping?"

"Yes, beekeeping. It was mostly a hobby, but we also sold the different flavored honeys we made at flea markets; all of our proceeds went to the Madison Square Boys and Girls Club. We had quite a little business going for a while. Anyway, the museum was looking for a board member with a legal background, so it was a natural fit for me."

"I see. So, Broadway-worthy drag shows, pro-bono legal work, beekeeping, philanthropy, museum board member... tell me, Francey, is there anything you don't do?"

"Well, Francey's answer would be 'encores,' because you always have to leave them wanting more," he jokes, then adds gently, "but like I told you before, please call me Francis when I'm not in drag."

"My mistake, Francis, but about that... are you really sure you're comfortable with your... " I search for a delicate way to put it, *"lifestyle* being publicized?"

His deep-set eyes look straight into mine and he replies, "Athena, I came to terms with who I am a long time ago."

"How's that?" I ask.

"My family is *extremely* conservative. So I learned from a young age how and when to be the good Jewish boy they wanted me to be, and the flaming dancing queen that *I* needed to be. Don't get me wrong, I have scars. My parents won't acknowledge any of my successes, and from the day I came out in seventh grade until high school graduation, I was teased and bullied mercilessly. Yet as horrible as it was, it made me strong, it made me successful. As far as your column goes, I have absolutely nothing to hide, because the truth is, I like who both of those people have evolved into."

He smiles and says in a theatrically high pitched voice, then low pitched voice, "The award-winning drag queen who packs the house every weekend with her over-the-top cabaret, and the award-winning civil rights attorney who kicks ass and takes names."

He takes a glass of wine from the server passing by, while I politely decline.

"You see Athena, sexual preference is not a choice; I am a gay man twenty-four hours a day, take me or leave me. However, the artistic medium through which I choose to express my sexuality is something completely different. Performing in drag is what I do, what I love to do, in fact, but it doesn't define who I am. Same goes for being an attorney. I don't bring the lawyer to the drag show or the drag queen to the courtroom, or to the museum for that matter, because there is no place for one in the other.

"Francey has her world, Francis has his. And the two shall never collide." He places his glass on the white linen tablecloth so his fingers are free to act out a graceful explosion. "We all wear different hats in our lives. I just take it to the extreme in mine. Do you know what I mean?"

I nod, recalling his bedazzled beret.

"I do. And I think whatever hat you wear, it's going to look perfect," I say. "Now, I'm curious, what kind of hat do you wear when you're beekeeping?"

"Oh, that's a special hat. There's all this netting involved, and…"

We talk about the ins and outs of beekeeping, as well as a few more of his eccentric hobbies, until a man wearing round glasses and a very obvious toupee, notices Francis and extends him a firm handshake with one hand, while serving himself from the platter of smoked salmon with the other.

"Howie, so good to see you! Athena, this is a close friend of mine and fellow board member, Dr. Howard Klein. He is *the* cosmetic dentist in New York."

"That means I do all the celebrity's veneers," he says with a chuckle. "I would offer you my card, but unfortunately I see that you have very beautiful teeth."

"Thank you, Dr. Klein, it's a pleasure to meet you," I say, shaking his hand.

"Please, call me Howie."

"Athena is a columnist for *The Socialite*, and I'm flattered to say she is going to be writing a piece starring yours truly."

"Well, you couldn't have picked a more interesting person than Francis," Howie says. "He is quite possibly the most well-rounded gentleman I know."

"I couldn't agree more, Howie. Anyhow, I have more than enough material, so I'm going to get going and let you two enjoy the exhibit." I say my goodbyes, and while embracing Francis I tell him, "Thank you so much for the opportunity to get to know you, and for the reminder that you can't judge a book by its sequined cover." He laughs and suggests that I use this metaphor in my story, verbatim.

I ask Taj to make a detour so I can grab a to-go container of vegetable chow mein, before arriving home to spend quality time with my laptop and furry slippers. The shoes were killing my feet, but I am not ready to give up the skirt just yet. Shoveling the chopsticks into my mouth, I skim all of the Wikipedia articles related to Viktor Frankl.

The first thing I learn is that he developed the psychotherapy called "logotherapy" to help himself and his patients survive the holocaust. It is based on the principal that the main motivation for living is the will to find meaning in life experiences. The word 'meaning' is reoccurring in my research of Frankl, and his focus on the search for meaning rather than the search for happiness is interesting to me.

With a few more clicks of the keyboard, I come across a quote of his that gives me pause. "It is the very pursuit of happiness that thwarts happiness." I open the linked article, in which Frankl goes on to say, "It is a characteristic of the American culture that, again and again, one is commanded and ordered to 'be happy.' Yet happiness cannot be pursued;

it must ensue. One must have a reason 'to be happy.'"

I repeat this over and over again in my head to allow it to sink in. *Happiness cannot be pursued; it must ensue. One must have a reason to be happy.* That reason is meaning. The sight of a greasy mushroom on my lap shakes me from my chain of thought. I rip my skirt off and run to the kitchen to blot the stain with dish soap and hot water. *Holy mother of shit. I'll never forgive myself for this.*

I say a little prayer over the silk lining as I hang it to dry over the bathroom towel rack, and my eyes begin to well up. *Really, Athena, just take it to the dry cleaner,* I tell myself, but at this point I have set in motion an avalanche of tears that have more to do with facing my unhappiness as of late than with ruined, overpriced couture. I think it is time to slip into my faithful cotton pjs and call it a night. My head needs to unwind from its recent breakthrough and breakdown, so I play Erykah Badu's "Didn't Cha Know" – you were made to make mistakes, but your heart will always guide you back in place – as I drift off to sleep.

*****

I duck into a dark alley to hide from the mob of Nazis chasing me. Terrified, I yell for help but no one can hear me because my words are in French. Suddenly, a Chinese star wizzes by my nose and Jackie Chan jumps out of a dumpster, wearing lace-up high-heeled boots.

"Wait here!" he shouts, as he runs through the fog after my pursuers.

In an instant, I am in the waiting room of a dentist's office, and the soothing music of Swan Lake is progressively being drowned out by the sound of a drill getting louder ... Louder .... LOUDER.

I snap up and pull back the velvet curtain behind my headboard to discover a construction crew digging up the road fifteen stories below. My first thought is, "why the hell are these guys working on a Sunday?" Immediately followed by, "crap it's Sunday!"

I check my phone to see that I have slept until almost ten o'clock, so I only have a few minutes to get ready to go to Lori's. Also staring up at me is a text message sent at 3:27 a.m.

Everything turn out ik?

My heart flutters and mind races. *Why was Anthony up that late? Did he go out instead of going home after he left the museum? If so, where and who with? Was his sloppy texting because he was drunk? I thought he didn't drink? Or maybe that's just around me. But why wouldn't he drink around me?*

Luckily, the rational side of my brain recognizes I do not have time right now to play this game, so I hop out of bed to brew a quick cup of coffee. As the amaretto creamer flows, I make note to never eat Chinese food and Google the holocaust before bed again.

*****

The commute to Lori's is short, and while the train weaves under Midtown Manhattan, my subconscious nags me to continue the internal dialogue about the happiness/meaning relationship. I promise it I will pick up where we left off again soon. Today I am taking a break from myself to enjoy time with the girls.

"Looks like someone had a long night!" I am taunted as I walk through the door.

"Nadine, it's too early in the morning for you to start this shit. I was up late with my laptop and no one else." I ignore her heavy sigh and shout to Lori in the kitchen, "Something smells good! What you fryin' up in there?"

She emerges with what appears to be a light dusting of flour in her hair, carrying a tray of three champagne flutes.

"Athena, you made it! I'm trying out a new recipe, I think you're really going to like it!"

Nadine discreetly shoots me a concerned look. I love Lori to death, but it is no secret the girl does not know her way around a kitchen. Lord knows she tries, though. She joins us on the oversized sectional and hands us each a mimosa.

"Oh, thank God!" Nadine exclaims. "When you said 'come for breakfast' I was worried there wasn't going to be any alcohol."

"Girl, you know me better than that."

We clink glasses and I almost choke as a big piece of pulp lodges itself in my throat.

"Freshly squeezed?"

"Of course!" Lori boasts.

I take a big swig in an attempt to wash it down and ask, "Where's Michael this morning?"

"At the gym. I tried to convince him to join us but he's been on this new diet lately. Poor thing. I rarely see him eat anything anymore but he just seems to keep gaining weight."

I hope she does not notice the light bulb go off over my head, as I recall running into him leaving McDonald's on my walk home from work a few months ago. He pleaded, as chunks of Big Mac flew out of his mouth, for me not to tell his wife that I saw him. At the time, it struck me as a bit suspicious and a lot disgusting, but now it all makes sense.

The thought also occurs to me that our last couple of get-togethers have been very Athena-centric, so I make an attempt to divert the attention away from my life for a change.

"So, Lor, how is married life, anyway? I've heard the first year can be a little challenging. Has reality set in, or is the honeymoon not over yet?"

"No, it's not over," she says, smiling. "Our love is strong and our souls are as one… but there is one small thing that's been weighing on my conscience. You know Michael loves kids and wants one of his own, like, *yesterday*, but I've been thinking a lot lately about going to nursing school.

It would be a lateral move money wise, but my spirit is starting to suffocate in the lab. I yearn for that human element, to interact with patients and to be part of their healing, not just their diagnosis. I looked into it, and the hospital offers a really great tuition assistance program... I don't know. I've been keeping this from Michael because I know how much he has his heart set on starting a family right now. He doesn't even know I'm still taking the pill." She exhales slowly. "I really don't think I could handle work, school, and a baby."

"Well I think you should go for it! Please talk to him about it. You're kind, and empathetic, and *smart*. Nursing would be perfect for you! Plus you're still young, there's lots of time for baby making down the road. I mean, there is, right? You've already got the father picked out so you're way ahead of me. Do you guys think I should consider freezing my eggs?" They both stop sipping their mimosas and look at me like I am crazy. There goes my attempt to not talk about myself.

"Never mind. What I meant to say is that you deserve to do something you love, and the baby thing can definitely wait while you pursue it."

"I agree. Now's the time. It's still doable with kids, but trust me, they make everything so much harder. So. Much. Fucking. Harder," Nadine says, her eyes lost in the paisley tapestry that hangs on the living room wall.

"I know, I'll talk to him. One of these days," Lori replies.

A timer beeps in the kitchen, and I attempt to bring Nadine back to earth while Lori goes to check on whatever is in the oven.

"What about you Nay, ever think about going back to school?"

"Girl, please. And leave the exciting world of office management?" I laugh as she fans her hands out. "No, I'm serious! My husband's the boss, I have it made. A quick BJ in the supply closet buys me a three-hour lunch and enough petty cash for a mani and pedi. I'm not rocking that boat."

"You're crazy."

"Okay, ladies, I hope you're hungry!" Lori yells from the kitchen. We exchange wide-eyed expressions and move to the pedestal table in her dining room. "I want your honest opinion," she insists as she slaps a large pile of an egg-like substance onto my plate. I am about to take a miniscule taste when Nadine throws down her fork with a loud clang.

"Alright, enough of this bullshit."

"What?" Lori and I both ask, perplexed.

"She's been here for almost half an hour and Miss Socialite hasn't said jack-diddly-do-dah about the last *two* Saturday nights she's spent with her photo *friend*. What are you hiding from us?"

"Jesus, Nay. I'm not hiding anything. Nothing. It's just been work. And his name is Anthony."

"I'm just saying, you were all excited about this new assignment before it started and I haven't heard shit about it since. So spill." She crosses her arms.

"Fine, but I assure you it's not the scandal you're hoping for."

I give the girls the abridged version, during which I am interrupted with, "*Open Arms*? Didn't that tall glass of hot chocolate sing that on season two of *The Voice*?" and "Only Athena would find a drag queen whose after-hours life is more boring than hers."

"I take offense to that, Nay. Francey was very interesting. And it wasn't after- hours, it was only, like, nine o'clock."

"Exactly."

"Anyway, I want you to know that I took to heart what we talked about that night on my balcony. You know, my quarter-life crisis? Okay, maybe more like my slightly-past-quarter-but-not-even-close-to mid-life-crisis? I think writing this series about the lives of complete strangers is helping me gain some perspective on my own life. I mean, I'm not even close to being there yet, but it's provoked me to start asking myself the kinds of questions that I think may lead me in a more positive direction."

"I think that's wonderful, Athena!" Lori exclaims. "It makes total sense. Sometimes you have to look outside of yourself to understand what's going on inside. I thought I sensed a change in your energy today."

"Sounds like some *Eat, Pray, Love* shit to me. Or in your case, *Drink, Work, Masturbate*."

I suck my teeth at Nadine.

"Girl I'm just playin'. I'm happy for you too. I think a change is way overdue in your life, so whatever you have to do to get there, I support. I only harass you about Anthony because I genuinely believe there's the potential for something real. Think about all you have in common. You're two single – wait, have we confirmed his relationship status?"

"No," I respond flatly.

"See, that's what Facebook stalking is for, Athena! I've been trying to tell your stubborn, dusty ass to get into this technological decade! You finally open a MySpace account and the rest of the world has moved on to Facebook. What do you even do all day at work without it?" Nadine throws her arms in the air. "You know what? It doesn't even matter if he's single.

"You're two hot, thirty-something, well-dressed, educated, successful people, who share the same professional interests and, as fate should have it, employer. So can I ask you a question? Do you like him?"

"Honestly? I'm not sure. Am I attracted to him? Hell yes! But I don't really know him like that. We haven't talked all that much, outside of work stuff. He's a man of few words. Plus, I promised myself I wasn't going to get all worked up over him. You know I have a history of falling too hard, too fast, and I just don't have it in me to have my heart broken right now."

"Why are you being so self-defeating with this man?" Nadine asks, vexed. "No one is saying you have to go all psycho over him and jump right into the deep end, but you can at least dip your toes in and test the waters. See if there's the potential for something. Why can't you just ask him out?"

"Because, Nay, I have to work side-by-side with him for at least the next month. What if he's not interested? Or what if we go out and it doesn't work out? That would be extremely awkward and would affect the quality of my column for sure."

"Okay, we get that, but say you don't actually *ask* him out. I mean, you're already out, right?' Lori asks.

"Riiight... What are you saying, Lor?"

"You make the rules. Just bend them in your favor."

"Huh?"

"I think I know where she's going with this Athena, and it's fucking genius!" Nadine proclaims.

"Well fill me in then."

"For your next night spot, you'll take him to a place where the ambience lends itself to romance," Lori says.

"That's dripping with sex appeal," Nadiney adds.

"I'm not taking him to a strip club."

"No, not a strip club...a place that has smooth music – "

"Jazz," Nadine interjects, "and that serves upscale cocktails – "

Lori doesn't skip a beat, "Wine, definitely red wine."

" ...with a swanky vibe..."

"A sophisticated crowd."

"...that feels intimate..."

"Mood lighting."

"Yes! With the little lamps on the tables!"

"*Suede!*" they declare in unison.

"I'm so glad you two have it all planned out, but this is work, not a date, remember?"

"Suede is the best jazz lounge in the city. If you recall, I was with you the last time you reviewed it. You're sure to meet some really cool bohemian there to write your column about," Lori says. "So the decision's been made. You're going to Suede next Saturday. All you have to do is talk to him, Athena. The mood is right, so if there's something there, you'll feel it. If not, we won't mention his name again. Now eat your breakfast before it gets cold."

Not even halfway through Sunday brunch, my efforts to stop monopolizing conversations and stressing over Anthony have both gone out the window.

"I'm going to put a pot of coffee on. Who wants a cup?" Lori asks, scooting her chair away from the table.

"I'm good. I'm percolating myself over here with all this sexy talk."

I shake my head at Nadine. "So Nasty, Nay."

"No coffee for me, but I will take a refill," I say as I raise my flute.

Lori disappears back into the kitchen and I call after her, "What do you call this dish again?"

"It's a kale and Portobello casserole. I bought the ingredients from a new co-op market that I joined. The eggs were so fresh, and for only a dollar for a dozen, can you believe it?"

"Yeah cuz, this is good," Nadine shouts as she spits her food into a napkin. "You really put your foot in this one!"

I frantically mash mine up and push it around the plate to make it look like I ate some. After last night's stain drama, mushrooms are on my shit list anyway.

Two mimosas later, we greet Michael as he strolls in with a gym bag over his shoulder. "Hey sweetie, how was your workout?" Lori asks as he bends down between her and Nadine to kiss them each on the cheek.

"Oh, it was a tough one today. My trainer took no prisoners. I'm gonna be hurting tonight!"

"I bet," I say under my breath. Nadine and I take this as our cue to go.

On my way to put my plate into the sink, which is crammed with an exorbitant amount of dishes and utensils used to prepare our meal, I brush past Lori and whisper, "Talk to him, please."

"I will. Thanks for coming over. I'm really proud of you for what you're doing with your column. Embarking on this new spiritual journey. It's going to be so worth it, I can feel it," she replies, her eyes sparkling.

"I hope you're right, Lor."

*****

On our walk together to the subway, Nadine asks, "Girl, is it just me, or did Michael's sweat smell like fried chicken?"

"Oh honey, that wasn't sweat!" I explain the man's secret love affair with Colonel Sanders, Ronald McDonald, and Lord knows who else, and after we share a belly laugh, Nadine turns serious.

"Athena, I know I always get on your case about finding a man, because I really do believe that marriage, and all the stuff that comes with it, makes life more complete. But you and Lori got me thinking today. When she was talking about how much Michael wants a baby, and when you were telling us the story about the drag queen, the whole 'don't judge a book by its cover' thing you're going to write about?" I nod and she continues.

"Last Friday the kid's were having a sleep over at their grandmother's house, and George and I were supposed to go on a date. Well, I came home a little drunk from our girl's happy hour and we ended up getting into it pretty bad. Screaming, name-calling, all of it. And do you know what the best part of us fighting was? It was that night. I know you think I mean make-up sex, but I don't. It was because George slept on the couch and I got the whole bed to myself. I got to spread out and sleep for eight glorious hours without being woken up by his loud ass snoring or a kid's foot in my ass. I woke up feeling so *refreshed*. You know, sometimes I'll even pick a fight with him so I can have a night like that?

"Now don't get me wrong, I wouldn't trade my family for the entire world. But as much as I want to see you in a long-term relationship, in the meantime I want to see *you enjoy you*. It's precious time you can't fully appreciate now, but will never get back. You understand?"

"I understand." We hug before descending the subway stairs.

"You only get to go down this road once. Promise me that while you're out there looking for happiness, you'll remember that the journey itself is a gift."

"Okay, Nay, I will," I assure her as we part ways. The whole way home, I meditate on her words. As funny and raunchy as Nadine is, she also can be very wise. *And I will*, I assure myself.

My soul is rested after spending the day with the girls, and when I arrive back at my loft I am not ready to lose the feeling. I have a fleeting urge to reply to Anthony's text from last night, but decide it would just be weird now since it is so late in the day. I hit the power button on the BlackBerry, and spend the rest of my Sunday in a warm, amber scented bubble bath with D'Angelo and a pile of trashy magazines. In the spirit of Frankl, I shall call this *Athenatherapy*.

*****

I decide to "work from home" the following day, and spend most of it indulging in another type of therapy: retail. The luxury of a flexible schedule is my reward for sacrificing every single Saturday night of my thirties thus far to my column. Sure, I am out and about, but it is usually more business than pleasure. Although, if my meddling friends have it their way, that will not be the case this week.

Upon arriving to the office Tuesday morning, the sight of Anthony sitting in my desk chair almost makes me pee a little in my new cashmere pants. Thank God I do not. They were sixty percent off, but still, I cannot afford another fashion calamity.

"Finally! When I didn't get a text back from you on Saturday or find you here yesterday, I was worried you were being held against your will. Like, forcibly gluing rhinestones onto polyester costumes in some sort of drag queen trafficking ring. Glad to see you're alive."

He's glad that I'm alive! "I made it out, but I barely escaped with my Louie." I sway my shoulder bag side to side, then ask how he is feeling.

"Much better, thank you. I told you it was just a little cold."

I pick up the disk of photos from my desk.

"Too bad I didn't get any photos of Francey out of drag," Anthony says.

"That's fine, I'm sure the ones from Wild Horses are great. I do wish you could have stayed, I mean, to take photos and to hear more of his story. Turns out there was an even more beautiful person under the mountain of foundation and red lipstick."

"Do you have a plan for this weekend yet?" he asks with that sexy smile on his face.

Well, I'm thinking a bed and breakfast Upstate, followed by an early morning hike to watch the sunrise, then back to the room to have passionate sex all day long, spanking is optional but strongly recommended, with only a brief interlude to refuel over a private candlelit dinner.

"Suede. Ever been there?"

"I have not. What kind of place is it?"

"It's a jazz club in Harlem. Really swanky, and with a lot of history. They say that Duke Ellington used to go there after playing at The Cotton Club because he preferred their brand of whiskey. If the mood struck, he'd put on a free show. There are not many authentic jazz clubs in the city anymore, they've all become so sterile and commercialized, but not this place, it's the real deal. So, um, I want to spotlight it." Not sure why I feel the need to over-justify my choice, like he is going to walk into the place and instantly see right through my, or should I say Nadine and Lori's, intentions. "Meet you there around, say, nine o'clock?"

"Alright, I'm more of a blues man myself, but I can dig it. Anyway, I have to run to do a style shoot for Larry. Good luck with your article."

"Bye Anthony, thanks for dropping this off and coming to check on me."

"Anytime," he promises as he closes the office door behind him. The intercom comes alive without skipping a beat.

"Mmmm hmmmm," says Mark.

"Can I help you, dear?"

"You can get me a date with his gay brother," Mark implores.

"I heard he's an only child. Anything else?"

"Nope, that is all." It clicks off and I am alone with my thoughts. Which I refuse to consume with a man, when it is already Tuesday, and all I have done is a rough outline for the Wild Horses review. I wake up my computer and inner journalist and get to work.

The closing words "by its sequined cover" do not reach the page until five minutes before deadline on Friday. *Phew.* Between taking Monday off, the nightlife news blog monopolizing most of my time over the last three days, and the challenge of ensuring my words did Francey and Francis justice, it is an unprecedentedly close call to get my column in on time this week.

The sound of activity in my inbox also allows me to breathe a sigh of relief. The Jewish Museum has finally gotten back to me with an official photo of their new exhibit. I attach it to an email along with a vibrant panoramic shot of Wild Horses, in the center of which is Francey doing a high kick with sparks exploding from her bosom. Once everything is en-route to editing, it is straight home to get some much needed beauty sleep.

Happiness Amongst the Naked?

Happiness Amongst the Naked?

CHAPTER 5

Smell is the first of my senses to come alive as I open the door to Suede. The air is thick with Nag Champa from an incense stick that burns between the metal clasps of an absent bass player's music stand.

I imagine the smoke floating through the room is the lingering haze from Duke's cigarettes, embodying the ghosts of the Harlem Renaissance and the chords of the golden age of jazz. With its black and white damask suede walls, solid mahogany bar, emerald fabrics, and rose gold crystal chandeliers, the space is reminiscent of the forgotten time of supper clubs, pocket watches, and pearls. Lori is always telling me I am an old soul, and if that is true, I must have spent a lot of time in a place like this, drinking mint juleps and dancing the night away in a silk evening gown.

Whether it is the sounds of John Coltrane or Charlie Parker, my untrained ear cannot decipher, but my soul is dizzied by the wailing of a saxophone on a melancholy solo. Touch is next. Fingers delicately trace the small of my back, leaving me close to breathless. It is Anthony. The girls were right, whether I decide to follow their advice or not. This is the perfect backdrop for a torrid rendezvous.

Anthony stands upon noticing my entrance, with an unnecessary wave to get my attention.

"Wow, you look great! I wasn't sure if I'd be over dressed, but now I'm glad I went with the suit." *Ah, yes.* The infamous designer suit he wore the day he landed the job that brought him here. A brown polka dot tie set against a powder blue shirt compliments his exquisite jacket, where light gray pin stripes faintly slice through an indigo sea that I would like to dive into to cool off. *You're just testing the waters*, I remind myself. *Easy breezy.* But 'easy' seems more doable. Literally.

I want to respond to his compliment with "this old thing?" but that hardly seems reasonable, seeing that I took the better part of the day trying on every dress in my wardrobe, at least three times, before finally going with this one from the special occasion section. A decision I still questioned up until this moment. Instead, I simply smile and take a seat, as a much easier choice is asked of me.

"A glass of pinot noir, please. Beaux Frères if you have it."

"Ahh, a lady of excellent taste," remarks the bartender, who is sporting a felt fedora and thin, gray plaid suspenders.

"You don't stick to one drink do you? There's no Athena signature cocktail?" Anthony asks.

"I have my favorites, but I usually like to match my drink to my environment. You know, to set the tone."

"I see. And this environment is pinot noir?"

"Very. Cranberry juice?" I allude to his drink of choice.

"Of course."

"I take it you don't like alcohol?"

"I do, but never when I'm working. I wouldn't want to... over indulge." I find his choice of words interesting. He must be referring to my antics during our first encounter. Ugh, the memory still haunts me.

Reminded of the official reason of this encounter, I take out my BlackBerry and see that I have two missed calls from Nadine and a text.

Crisis. Call me.

Panicked, I excuse myself and turn away to return her call. "Nay? It's me. What's wrong?"

"Oh girl, thank God you called! I'm having a crisis."

"Crisis? What kind of crisis. You okay? George and the kids?"

"It's just awful. I'm having a vagina crisis. It's the worst case of sympathy horniness you've ever seen. My panties are soaked."

I frantically push the phone's volume button down with my left hand, and cup the mouthpiece with my right hand.

"Nadine!"

"Athena, I know you girl, I know you well. Right now, you are sitting next to that fine specimen of a man, debating whether or not to do what Lori and I told you to do. Well I'm going to make it reeeal simple for you and tell you the answer is 'yes.' Do it. Let your fucking hair down and flirt your fucking ass off. For your benefit, not his. Enjoy yourself. Remember? What are you wearing anyway?"

"My red Oscar de la Renta cocktail dress," I whisper.

"Good, but I can tell from here you need to push it up in the boobs and down in the back." I shift uncomfortably in my seat.

"Anything else miss bossy pants?"

"No. Now get off the phone with me and for a few short hours, stifle the boring ass journalist side of you and set the fun, confident Athena that I know is in there with her moist panties on, free."

"Ew!"

"Goodbye," she purrs.

"Bye!" I huff. Flushed, I return first to my wine, then to Anthony.

"Everything all right?"

"Yes, fine. My friend was just having a minor crisis, but it's been resolved."

"Glad to hear. So, do you have any idea about who to approach in here?" As he turns his head to peruse the modest crowd, I quickly and discreetly adjust my dress according to Nadine's instructions. I guess the decision has been made. *Now what?*

"I don't know yet. I was thinking of approaching one of the band members. They'd probably have some valuable feedback about this place, and I imagine the life of a musician could be pretty interesting."

"Sounds like a plan. Do you know who's playing?" he asks.

"No, but I bet he does." I signal to the young man under the hat. "Excuse me? Can you tell us who the band is tonight?"

"The Scat Cats, from nine to one, then their bass player sticks around and plays 'til close." He glances at his watch, a striking piece that, upon further inspection, appears to be an antique Rolex.

"They already warmed up so should be starting anytime now. Ever seen them before?" We shake our heads. "Lucy, the lead singer, has killer pipes. If you close your eyes you'd swear you were in the presence of Sarah Vaughan. Should be a good show."

I thank him, and before I can stress over having to make small talk, the band trickles on stage.

Other than a "they sound good" here and "I like this song" there, Anthony and I do not talk much for the next hour. By the time the band takes their first break, most of the tables of two that sit between the stage and us have become occupied. A cocktail waitress weaves through the maze of the tightly packed chairs, serving drinks to close talking couples.

The band joins us at the nearly vacant bar to retrieve the pitcher of beer that awaits them. To my surprise, Anthony takes the lead this time.

"Great set, guys. Loved your cover of *Summertime*. Can we buy you a shot to accompany that beer?" They all agree, and while taking a head count for the order, he points to me. I am tempted to shave a bit more of the edge off, but, still gun-shy, respectfully decline. "Six royal flushes please," Anthony tells the bartender.

"Aren't you two going to do one?" Lucy asks, as she picks up her shot.

"No, we're actually here on assignment for *The Manhattan Socialite*. I'm Anthony, and this is Athena."

They raise their glasses to us before downing the blood red shot. The piano player and male vocalist/trumpeter take their beers down the bar to huddle over a sheet of music, while the sax player leaves to join a friend in the audience. It is the bassist, a middle-aged man with dreadlocks and a bushy beard, who steps forward to shake our hands.

"Thanks for the drinks. My name's Roland, I'm the band manager. Are you here to write a review on us or on Suede?"

"Suede," I answer. "But I'll be sure to pass on to our music columnist how great you guys are. Do you have a business card?" He pats his shirt and pant's pockets but comes up empty. "Hey Lucy, you have one of our cards for them?" She shakes her head, and returns to her conversation with the drummer. "Sorry about that. But you can find all of our info on our website, Scat Cats jazz dot com."

I type the address into my BlackBerry. "Roland, would you mind answering a few questions about Suede for our story? We're naming it best jazz lounge in the city. I'd be interested in getting their input too." I point to the two women, and Roland calls Lucy and Shawn over. They are friendly enough; however, all three seem reluctant to give more than a one or two word answer to my questions.

"How many times have you played at Suede?"

"Seven."

"What's the best part of performing here?"

"Guaranteed crowd."

"What sets them apart from other clubs you play?"

"The atmosphere."

"Do any of you come here when you're not working?"

"Sometimes."

Really?

"Look, we've got to go over a few things before we're back on. Thanks again for the shots." Roland whistles to the sax player and they head to the other end of the bar to join the two men debating over the pages strewn in front of them. Reluctant to let them slip through my fingers as potential subjects, I follow.

"Hey, wait, we're not only doing a review here tonight. We're also looking to do a biography of sorts on how a New York musician, or even a band, spends a Saturday night in the city, after their gig. Is that something any of you would be interested in?"

Six heads shake unhesitatingly and Roland replies, "Enjoy the rest of the show."

Confused and a little offended, I return to my seat. "Was that weird or is it just me? Why wouldn't they want free publicity?" My questions are directed to Anthony, but answered by our bartender, who is nearby, filling orders for the waitress and apparently eavesdropping.

"It's not that they don't want publicity. They're probably afraid that if they go on the record promoting this place, they'll piss off the other spots they play. The bar business is super competitive in this city, and so is landing a good gig. I don't blame them for not wanting to take the risk. Plus, you know how uptight those musician types can be." He playfully rolls his eyes while aggressively shaking a martini. "But I'll do it."

"Excuse me?" I ask.

"I'll do it. I'll help you with your column."

"I appreciate it, but you're working, and we're really looking for – "

"A New York musician, I know. I'm a musician. Aspiring, obviously. When my shift ends at eleven, I'm headed to a gig. You can follow me if you'd like."

"All right," I say, feeling good about his easy vibe. "Thanks for volunteering –?"

"Theo. I'll top off your drinks while you wait."

The Scat Cats play an up-tempo second set, during which Anthony and I say even less to each other than in the first. A pretty blonde arrives to relieve Theo from his shift. He pours himself a Bombay Sapphire on the rocks and comes around the bar to sit with us and count the crumpled bills the waitress tossed in his tip bucket.

"Hey man, I forgot to pay for the shots. How much do I owe?" Anthony asks.

"No, put it on my tab, I'll settle it right now," I say, reaching for my wallet.

"No worries, I already picked it up. You guys are doing *me* a favor."

"What do you mean?" I ask.

"Well, Athena, I wouldn't call myself a starving artist, as much as a hungry one. But just like the thousands of other people in this city, I'm impatiently waiting to be famous."

I start typing. "Tell us more about yourself, Theo."

"Well, I work seven days a week at Suede, which, by the way, is owned by my father. He bought it a few years back from the grandson of the original owner, who was looking to get out of the bar business when the recession hit. My dad didn't care about the money; he owns one of the top jazz record labels in the country. The bar's more of a hobby for him, and he hasn't changed one thing about it since taking over. It's sentimental to him here – it's where he discovered the first artist he ever signed to his label."

"I don't understand. If your father's in the industry, why doesn't he just hook you up?" I ask.

"Ah, if it were only that simple. Not only will he not give me a job in music, he refuses to even introduce me to anyone in the business. It's personal for him. My dad came from nothing. He was brought up poor and had a father who used to beat the shit out of him every chance he got, so when he wasn't at school, he was at a job scrubbing slaughterhouse floors in the Meatpacking District. Saved every penny and put himself through school. Got a Master's Degree in Entertainment Business Management.

He thinks because he had to do things the hard way, the 'right' way, I should too. But I was never good at school. I'm dyslexic, and shit got too hard in high school, so I dropped out my sophomore year. He never even tried to understand why. Just kicked me out of the house, and told me I wasn't welcome back until I learned how to follow the rules."

"That's rough, man," Anthony says.

"Yeah, well, that's his style," Theo replies, cracking his knuckles as he speaks.

"You were just a kid. Where did you go? How did you get by?" I ask.

"I packed up my guitar and notebook and took a bus to L.A. I played every street corner I came across and bought one meal a day with the change people tossed in my case. It was the first time I was away from my parent's cushy lifestyle in the Jersey burbs, so living like that got super old, fast. I met a group of guys at the hostel where I slept who connected me with a small time grass dealer. I just wanted to make a little bit of money to buy some new equipment so I could get a real gig, but it only took a few weeks before I was busted. I was facing jail time, but my dad knew a judge out there and somehow got the charges reduced to a misdemeanor. He flew out to California to get me, and we didn't say one word to each other the whole way home. In fact, we didn't speak for months.

"My father never laid a hand on me, but sometimes I wished he would. I wish he would break the brutal silence and end the fight. I was allowed back in the house, but only if I enrolled in classes and worked as a janitor at his office building. He thought that would teach me some kind of lesson about starting at the bottom. I eventually got my GED and that put us on speaking terms... I noticed you checking out my watch earlier. It was a sort of a sort of a peace offering from him. He bought it with his first royalty check. It's the only thing from my dad's career he's ever passed down to me..."

Theo swirls his glass, his eyes lost in the whirling gin for a few moments before he continues. "You know, the funny thing is, I always suspected my dad was jealous of me. Of my talent. He loves the music business so much but can't play a damn note. Meanwhile, I learned to play the untouched baby grand in our living room by ear when I was seven.

"By ten, I had moved on to string instruments, and at thirteen mastered the horns..." He looks up at me from his drink and adds, "Please don't print that part though, about him being jealous of me. I don't care if people know about me living on the streets or selling drugs, those are mistakes I own up to, but I really don't want to start shit back up with my dad.

"Anyway, it's water under the bridge, at least for now. He offered me the bartending job here a year ago. I make enough in tips that I can finally afford my own place. It's a run-down studio in a shitty neighborhood, but I'm only there when I'm sleeping. When I'm not here, I work every gig I can find, I don't care what it is. As long as I'm playing my music and someone's listening. You never know when that one person is in the audience who could change your life."

My fingers have been fiercely typing, and by the time they are able to catch up, he has to shout over the start of the Scat Cats' third set.

"Why don't you guys follow me out back? I don't want to be late."

I tell Anthony and Theo I will be right there, then dash to the ladies room to do the standard hair and makeup check and ensure my outfit is still in place. It is; however, the inside of my mouth and lips are stained crimson from the wine. Damn, that's not sexy. Thankfully, I never leave home without my travel toothbrush, a necessary accessory for a wine addicted journalist. I exit out the front and walk the perimeter until I find Theo leaning against the brick wall of the alleyway. A saxophone case is propped up beside him, and he's smoking.

"Your friend will be right out. He said he had to take some photos inside." He exhales a big cloud as I hear the click of Anthony's wingtips coming up behind me. I brace myself to be disgusted as the smoke wafts toward me, but instead of the dirty tar smell I am expecting, my nose is met with a sweet musty odor that instantly takes me back to my freshman year dorm room.

"You guys want to hit this before we go?" Before I have the chance to even consider it, to my complete and utter shock, Anthony reaches for the joint.

"You don't mind Athena, right?" *What the... ? I thought he didn't "indulge" while working!*

"Not at all," I respond, attempting to strip my voice of its bewilderment. Anthony closes his eyes and takes the longest, sexiest drag a joint has ever experienced. *Lord have mercy.* Standing there in his suit, smoking, he looks like the suave leading man in an old black and white movie.

"Smooth," he comments, then offers it to me. My first inclination is to pass, but Nadine's words fill my ears. *Enjoy yourself.* So I do.

The rolling paper is slightly wet from his saliva, and this turns me on in the worst way. I inhale deeply and am treated to a rich, multi-dimensional flavor that swells in my lungs and warms me from the inside out. My anxieties take the form of various shapes and colors as they escape my body and float through the crisp night air. This is not the stuff I smoked in college.

"I'm no weed connoisseur, but this shit is delicious," I say. Anthony laughs and Theo takes it from between my fingertips.

"What you're tasting is a 2013 medium bodied hydroponic blend imported from Oregon, that has been slightly aged in a plastic sandwich bag. Earthy notes of oak and burnt vanilla highlight the grassy flavor, accompanied by an herbal bouquet of orange zest and clove."

He adds while inhaling, "Jazz musicians get the best pot." With the exception of a hint of mint toothpaste, his description is dead on. It must not be too potent though, because the only buzz I have is a remnant from the glass and a half of wine. I take one more hit and leave the rest of the joint for the guys to finish.

"Where's your gig anyway? I didn't think we'd need my cab driver all night, so we'll have to hail one."

"That's not a problem. We can take the subway to the Met."

"What's going on at the Met? Isn't it closed by now?" Anthony asks.

"Yeah, a group rented out one of the galleries to host an after-hours speed-dating party. They hired me to provide the background music."

"Nice. Sounds classy," I say, relieved not to be overdressed for another event at a museum.

"We should get going." Theo ashes the roach on the building, and leads the way to the nearest station.

Anthony stands on the train to let Theo and I sit together. The faint scent of sandalwood from Anthony's cologne is a stark and erotic contrast to the dank subway air. Eye level with his belt, I am trying my best not to look but I really want to.

"Look, Athena." Theo takes a tattered composition notebook from his case and hands it to me. "Since I won't be singing, I want to show you some of the lyrics to the songs I'll be playing tonight." He points to a few of the pages as I flip through. Most of them are about love and pain, ambiguous enough that I am not sure if he is referring to a woman or to something else entirely.

"Oh my God, Theo, there must be a hundred songs in here."

"One hundred and seven. The L.A. ordeal was horrible, but made for a songwriter's wet dream. And they aren't all necessarily jazz pieces either. I write music that can easily be transposed to different genres, like alternative rock or R&B. Any style that conveys emotion."

"Hey Anthony, could you take a picture of this book? You don't mind, right?"

Theo shakes his head. "Not at all, but please blur the songs a little. You can do that, right? Wouldn't want anyone stealing my shit."

"You got it," Anthony assures him.

After a few quick photos, I hand the notebook back and take out the BlackBerry.

"Earlier, you said you want to be famous. Can you qualify that for me? Describe your dream."

"Sure. My songs are based on what I've been through, and the composing process itself is very therapeutic. It helps me to understand situations better. Myself better. That notebook gives the darkest times of my life meaning, and I know it could do the same for others. My dream? My dream is to help people through my music. To give sound and rhythm and lyrics to an emotion a person couldn't name or didn't know what to do with or just needed to celebrate or let go of.

"To hear a song written by Theo and love with his heart, cry with his tears, heal with his wounds. To understand that someone else has gone through the exact same thing. That they're human. That's what music is really about, and it's my passion. It's my dream."

"That's really deep, Theo," I reply. And as the train arrives, so does my high.

At first, it starts off as a fuzzy sensation in my toes, then rises up, up, up to my cheeks. They must be red, because Anthony turns to me as we climb the stairs to the Metropolitan Museum of Art and says, "You're feeling it too, huh?"

"Yeah, I should have warned you guys about the pot. It has a bit of a delayed reaction," Theo says. "Don't worry though, it's nice and mild. You'll enjoy yourselves."

Well, that was the point, right?

I'm carefully concentrating on my feet – *don't trip, don't trip, don't trip* – and as we near the top step, Theo's Rolex swings into view. A suspicious thought occurs to me, and I stop dead in my tracks.

"Hold up. Why are they having this so late? What type of group is this, exactly?"

"You'll see. Come on," Theo says with a grin while holding the door open.

We follow the signs to the NAD NY speed-dating event. *Beavis and Butthead* pop into my head, and it is all that I can do to keep from giggling at the word 'NAD.' I wonder what it stands for. Night-owl Artist Daters? Newly Adulterous Dads? Nymphos After Dark?

We turn the corner into the Renoir wing, and a man wearing nothing but a whistle and a fanny pack scares the living crap out of me. I let out a tiny shriek as he greets Anthony and me, and hands us each a pamphlet.

"Welcome to the Nudist Association of Downstate New York's evening of speed-dating. Here's a list of the rules. You can de-robe over there. We've provided cubbies for your belongings, and towels to sit on." The naked man looks past us to Theo's saxophone case. "Oh, you must be the musician! Wait here while I get Peter."

With my jaw on the floor, I turn to Theo who is slipping off his suspenders and stepping out of his shoes.

"THEO!" I hiss.

"What? Are you mad I didn't tell you it's nude speed-dating? I thought it would be a fun twist for your story! This city's got everything, doesn't it? I'm getting naked, part of the contract, but I don't think you guys have to."

I have not had a chance to pick my jaw up when Mr. Poochpurse returns with another naked friend.

"I'm Richard, the event organizer, and this is your pianist, Peter." Laughter bursts out of my still-open mouth, while Anthony uses me as a shield to hide his snickering. Theo bends into his case to retrieve sheet music for Peter, and Dick spins around to glare at me. "I'm sorry, can I help you?"

Control yourself. Deep breaths. You are a professional journalist.

"I'm sorry, my, er, co-worker," I side step in order to use Anthony as a prop, "just told me a hilarious joke. You know the one about the two naked guys who walk into a bar and..." Still glaring. "No? Okay. Anyway. Hi. I'm Athena Wallace. I, we, are from *The Manhattan Socialite* and doing a story tonight on Theo, your song bird over here."

I do a Price is Right showcase reveal wave at Theo, who interrupts his conversation with Peter to reply, "Cah caw!"

"I see," Dick retorts, unimpressed. "You are most welcome to report on our event, but photos of the guests are strictly prohibited. And the museum does not allow the use of a flash." I lean into Anthony.

"Do you want to lea –"

"Hell no! I'm sticking around for this one!" he responds enthusiastically, as a curvaceous young woman struts by.

Yuck, wouldn't you groom yourself for an event like this? I won't even go to the corner store for a pack of gum if my eyebrows aren't properly plucked.

"Do we have to, you know, get naked?" I feel the need to lower my voice for the last word.

"Since you are with the press and not participating, I will say to do whatever makes you comfortable. As long as you allow others to feel the same." His glare intensifies.

"Understood. Will Do, Richard." More snickering from Anthony. I have to bite my lower lip to maintain my composure as I jab him in the ribs. Our host takes leave to welcome more naked guests, and Peter jiggles over to the piano bench. Theo, who now has one leg out of his pants, seems unfazed.

"So, what else do you need for your story?"

"Not that!" I close my eyes and point at the region his shirt is barely covering. "Would you please finish changing over there?"

He smiles devilishly and shuffles to the designated strip down area. The thought enters my mind that I was very wrong earlier. I am, in fact, extremely overdressed for this.

"We should stand in the back," a glassy-eyed Anthony suggests, as Richard clears his throat in the front of the room. More than two dozen small tables and chairs are lined up down the center, and about fifty ass cracks congregate around them to face the speaker.

"Hello? Can everyone hear me? Great, then let's get started. A big welcome to the semi-annual NAD singles midnight mixer!" I cover my mouth to stifle the giggle. That word is still funny. "Tonight we're trying something new, by speed-dating right here in the beautiful Renoir wing." I finally notice the nude paintings that surround us. "If you open the pamphlet you received, you'll find a sticker with your number on it. Please peel it off and stick it to your chest."

"That's going to hurt coming off," Anthony whispers.

I snort and nosedive into the rule book as Dick continues. "Gentlemen, if you would please sit in the chairs on the left side of the tables."

"Those towels are pretty thin, I hope they disinfect them later."

"Shhh!" I scold Anthony as I peek out. I do not want to look, but I have to.

"Tonight, the ladies will come to you. Ladies, please line up in no particular order in front of the men. When I blow this," his whistle drowns out the laugh that escapes, "you have five minutes to sit with a partner and get to know him. Suggested topics can be found in your book, along with a scorecard. When time's up, I'll blow it again, and you'll discreetly circle 'yes' or 'no' on the card to indicate whether you're interested in going on a real date.

"Make sure to note the number of the person you're sitting with, so when you get home, you can log onto the NAD website and click the speed-dating link. Enter the data from your card and presto!" He claps his hands and his junk slaps against his thigh. "You'll be matched to the daters who gave you a mutual 'yes.' Once everyone completes the survey, we'll send you an email with your matches and their contact information." This incites random applause.

"Before we get started, I'd like to introduce you to some very important people. My lovely wife Felicia, she's manning our refreshment table in the far corner." An overweight woman, whose boobs are sagging dangerously close to the punch bowl, waves as heads turn in her direction. "The museum has graciously granted an exception by allowing us to serve snacks and clear beverages. Please be very conscious to not spill any liquids, and place them in the proper receptacle when you are finished."

I am holding my breath and choking back the tears, as Anthony buries his face in his hands.

"Give a warm welcome also to Theo and Peter, who are here to provide some relaxing music for you all."

Theo stands to acknowledge his audience, and I see that the fedora is the only article of clothing that remains. Thankfully, the bell of his saxophone is appropriately positioned.

"Now that the introductions are out of the way, let's get started!" Richard blows his whistle and the vaginas sit down.

"I'll wait here if you want to grab a seat?" Anthony jokes. I finally catch my breath and slap his shoulder.

"No! We need to get out of here, now! If I see one more wrinkly ball or hairy butt crack I think I'm going to puke. Plus, I'm really hungry. Want to grab something to eat?"

He laughs at my ridiculous statement and responds, "Yes, I'm starving. Let me get a quick shot of Theo before we go."

I focus my eyes straight ahead as we walk past the exposed singles, and try desperately to keep a straight face when I overhear conventional small talk such as, "So, do you work out?" and "Long Island? Nice. How is it down there?"

Richard keeps careful watch on Anthony as he photographs only Theo, who seems to be enjoying the attention. It occurs to me I have forgotten to have him fill out a release form, so I impatiently wait for the song – a lovely piece – to come to an end. When it does, he reaches down for a pen. The saxophone shifts.

"Forget the address part! You can call or email it to me. Fax it if you want." I fumble though my purse for a business card, and flick it into the plush interior of the sax case. "Just sign it, here." Without diverting my eyes, I push the paper at him. I can tell by the amount of time his signature takes that Theo is amused by my discomfort. We turn to leave as he puts his mouth back on the instrument, but I remember one more thing.

"Wait! What's your full name?"

"Thelonius Wilson. Spelled like Thelonius Monk. T – H – E –" Curiosity gets the best of me as I reach to borrow the pen he has placed on his music stand and my eyes glance down. He sees me do it, and smirks. "Want another picture for yourself? A close-up, perhaps?"

"Forget it! I'll Google it!" Mortified, I spin around and drag a hysterical Anthony out by the arm.

We do not stop laughing until our waitress offers us coffee at the greasy spoon on 86th Street. I cover the mug before she can fill it.

"Do you have any amaretto creamer?" She looks at me like I am out of my damn mind, swirling the coffee in its pot impatiently. "I'll just have a very large water then." Anthony hands me a menu from the edge of the table and opens his.

"I'm really surprised you didn't participate back there. I mean, it's an ideal way to meet someone. What you see is what you get. *Everything's* out in the open." I smack him with my menu.

"Gross! Did you notice there was not one attractive person in there!" *Except for you of course,* I want to add. "God, I thought the euphemisms would never end."

"Me either. I can't believe Theo didn't tell us it was for nudists. Who would've guessed there are that many people in this city that get down like that! Good for them though. I envy their… openness."

"Ha! I guess. I can't imagine being that comfortable in my own skin."

"Really? You seem to be a very confident woman, and trust me, you look way better in that dress than any of those women did without clothes on."

A burning sensation rushes through me, and I think I am blushing from head to toe. I wish he would elaborate, but instead he shakes two sugar packets into his coffee and nonchalantly changes the subject.

"That dude did have some serious talent. Do you think he's going to remember to send you his info? It would suck if you can't use the story."

"I'm not worried about it. I got a signature, that's all that legal cares about. I agree with you about his talent, I hope we help him get some attention."

A small glass of water is set in front of me. No ice, no straw.

"I'll have the buttermilk pancakes with a side of hash browns, whole wheat toast with butter and raspberry jam, and, ummm, an order of cheese sticks." I am confused when Anthony hands her his menu.

"Oh, that was all for you?" he jokes. "Then I guess I'll have a bacon double cheeseburger, medium rare, with fries. And keep the waters coming, please." She huffs away, and I keep the conversation going. I am chatty on marijuana.

"And did you pick up on the fact that Theo was so concerned about having the photo of his notebook blurred, but didn't mention a thing about the pictures you took of him?"

"That's true... but you seemed to really enjoy the view."

I slap my forehead and fall back into the booth. "No, no, no. You misunderstand. I'm a journalist. It's my *job* to be inquisitive."

"Ooooh I see, it's your *job*!"

"Yes, it is... You know, you're usually pretty quiet. It's nice having a conversation with you," I say, the words falling out of my mouth before I can catch them.

"Well, thank you, it's nice having a conversation with you, too. To be honest, I've never been completely comfortable talking to women because I never spent a lot of time around them. So, maybe I come off as quiet at times."

I lean over the table and whisper to him, "The weed helps, doesn't it?" He answers with a delicious, crooked smile.

"So, I take it you were raised by men?" I say.

"Yeah, my pops was a single father of three boys. All of my grandmothers and aunties live down south, and I never met my mother; she up and left us when I was a baby. Being a family of all men, we were the exception to the rule in the neighborhood where I grew up."

"In the Bronx, right?"

"I see you've done your homework. We lived in Morris Heights, the projects where hip-hop was born. At least that's what they say. There was always music around; that, and violence. It was rough, but while all the other boys were picking up basketballs and criminal records, I picked up a camera."

"Who taught you about photography?"

"My pops actually bought me my first camera, a Polaroid on my ninth birthday. Man, that thing must have cost him half his paycheck, but he said he was tired of me burying my nose in the one family photo album we had from when my mom was still around. He told me to go out and take some new pictures, make some new memories. So I did, and I loved it. Made it my mission from then on to get out of the bricks, go to college, and become a professional photographer."

"I remember Brian saying you worked for *The R&B Beat* before coming to *The Socialite*. That's a big-time magazine, what made you leave?"

"You know, I'm starting to feel like I'm being interviewed for the next installment of *Come Here Often*. I'm not, am I?" he asks, slanting his brown and butterscotch eyes at me.

"No offense, Anthony, you're interesting and all, but your entertainment value pales in comparison to a jazz club bartender turned naked musician who plays for nudist speed-daters."

"Touché... To answer your question, my job at *The R&B Beat* was like a dream come true for me, at least in the beginning. I was immersed in my two passions, music and photography, day in and day out. Not only did I meet some really famous musicians, but I got to use my art to bring out a side of them that no one ever saw before. I was jet-setting constantly, living out of extravagant hotel rooms, and for awhile it felt like I was living someone else's life.

I saw concerts and countries that I could only dream about as a kid. So, when *The Socialite* approached me with the job, you'd think I wouldn't give it a second thought, right? Yet there was this part of me that craved stability, craved sleeping in the same bed every night and doing normal things like, grocery shopping or making Sunday dinner for my girlfriend."

My high is ripped away and replaced with crushing disappointment at the sound of the word 'girlfriend.' The chest pocket of Anthony's jacket lights up.

"Speak of the devil," he answers it, "Hey Renée... yeah, we're just finishing up. I'm about to grab some diner food, want anything?" The unpleasant waitress has returned with our order. "Excuse me miss, could I please have another bacon cheeseburger, to go?"

"You know, if you don't mind, could you wrap mine to go, too? Suddenly I'm really tired."

"Everything in doggie bags then?" She asks him, annoyed.

"I guess so, thanks so much. Put it all on here." He hands her his credit card.

"No, no, I can get mine," I open my purse but he reaches across the table to catch my arm.

"I insist."

"Okay," I respond softly, suffocating under the pressure of my Spanx. "I have to call Taj. Can you just meet me out front when it's ready?"

"Um, sure. You all right Athena?"

"Yeah, I'm fine." I force an unwilling smile. "Just need some fresh air."

The pain that is seeping through my body is not numbed in the least by the cold night air. *A girlfriend.* Of course he has a girlfriend! Why wouldn't he? He has far too much sex appeal and depth to be single. It could not, it would not, be that easy...

Thankfully, Taj is only a couple blocks away, and I am already in the backseat of the cab when Anthony emerges from the restaurant with my food. The yellow smiley face on the plastic bag mocks me as he passes it through the open window.

"Goodnight Athena. Tonight was fun! I can't wait to see what you write."

"Thanks. Night." I'm not even going to offer him a ride. He can walk his relationship having ass home to Renée. Their love can keep him warm.

Taj must pick up on my mood because he does not say a word as we pull away. I yank the BlackBerry out and text four words to my friends, rage surging through my thumb with each period I type.

He. Has. A. Girlfriend.

Then hit the off button because I do not want to talk about it. I just want to go to bed.

*****

With the exception of three trips to the bathroom, and one to the fridge to retrieve the Styrofoam container of soggy food, the bed is where I stay the entire next day. Just when I started to peek out from under it, I spiral back to the dark abyss inside of myself. The steel lid has been pushed over it so tight that no light can penetrate through. This is more than a feeling about a man. Does it suck that Anthony is taken? Hell yes. But even worse is that I allow one minor fact about someone else's life to weigh so heavily on me that it obliterates my self-worth. I feel ugly. Stupid. Empty. And dreadfully alone.

When I am all cried out from singing along to every Adele song on the iPod (twice), it is almost eight p.m. and begrudgingly time to turn the phone back on. I would not want anyone to think something awful had happened to me, even though it did. *Sigh*. Right away, five voicemails and three text messages pop up. All from Nadine and Lori, except for one call from my mother. Something about her hairdresser's single nephew who is a veterinarian. I will deal with her another day.

Oh no I'm soooo sorry.
Athena, where are you? Everything ok? Call me.
ATHENA PICK UP THE DAMN PHONE BEFORE I HAVE THE POLICE COME LOOK FOR YOU.

I place a three-way call so I only have to do this once.
"Girl, you had us worried sick! Don't you ever ignore us like that again!"
"Nay, I'm sorry. I didn't mean to scare you. I just needed some time to think."
"Think? Think about what? That the man has a girlfriend? I'm probably more disappointed than you are. But it's okay. You weren't even sure you liked him anyway, right? Better to find out now than later, when you might've had real feelings for him," Nadine tries to console me.
"Yeah, sweetie, I'm sorry if we pushed you into it. I wouldn't have been so persistent if his aura didn't have 'unattached' written all over it. I guess I was wrong," Lori says.
"You didn't push me. I would have found out eventually. The worst part is that we actually were having an amazing time until he mentioned it. We talked and laughed, we smoked weed…"
"You smoked weed! Damn. Good for you! If anyone needs to get high it's you," Nadine says. "But seriously Athena, please tell me you won't let this beat you down. You put yourself out there, tested the waters, and it sounds like you enjoyed it. So, take that attitude and move on to the next one."
"I know, Nay. Listen, I've had a busy day, and really just need to sleep. I'm sorry if I worried you girls."

"We're just glad you're all right. Call us when you're up for a happy hour," Lori says.

"You know I will. Love you both."

Nadine has the last word. "Bye, Snoop Lion."

I toss my phone on the nightstand and bury my head in the pillow. *All this drama over a guy? A guy I am not even dating? A guy who has the nerve to show up looking and smelling all kinds of good, complimenting my outfit, and being all charming and distracting when we are supposed to be working? A guy who had the audacity to assume I'm single by making a snarky comment about me joining the naked speed-dating party? ASS.* Anger does not mend the hole in my stomach, but it does save me from leaving the bed for more tissues.

*****

As tempting as it is to "work from home," another day spent hiding under 600 thread count Egyptian cotton will only make matters worse. I do not have the energy to stress over a deadline this week. So I find myself, yet again, staring through the mental fog at a blank page on my computer. Theo certainly gave me enough to write about, but I am struggling to find the inspiration today.

Hoping some jazz will put figurative pen to paper, I open Pandora and select the Billie Holiday station. As Lady Day croons "Glad to Be Unhappy" – a song about, what else, unrequited love – its relevance resonates. Unhappy. That about sums it up. Minus the "glad to be" part, of course. I cannot concentrate on my column until I attempt to tie up the loose ends that linger from it.

Come Here Often is halfway over. Three weeks, three very unique stories. The series has proved more compelling than expected, and I hope the momentum continues. Yet what about the personal side of this experiment? What have I learned from these experiences? Frustration got the best of me last time I was at this impasse, so I will start over. I will treat this like I would when working on any other assignment... I need to organize my thoughts. I need an outline. And I need to doodle on it.

I pull up *My Desires*, and begin typing whatever comes to mind as I reflect on the last three Saturdays. Words, thoughts, quotes. When I am finished, my page looks like this:

Week 1 - Vince:
<u>True romance should be simple/effortless</u>
Want = a thing, end in itself
Desire = involves an active commitment, similar to a goal, but with more emotion
Fulfillment/happiness = achieving desires??

Week 2 – Francey/Francis:
<u>Different hats, 1 person at core</u>
Don't judge a book by its cover
Happiness can't be pursued; must ensue
Happiness requires a reason; the reason is meaning (Viktor Frankl)
"Enjoy yourself, journey itself is a gift" (Nadine)

Week 3 - Theo:
<u>Paving own way, whatever it takes</u>
Smoke weed, enjoy self
Notebook, emotion, talent
Writing/music as therapy, healing, passion
Nudists!

Me:
<u>Had fun, until... girlfriend... depression</u>

Although I do not end on the most uplifting note, I do feel better having my thoughts in order. Now that they exist outside of my head, it is as if room has been freed up inside of it. I save the document, renaming it *My Reflections*, and create a shortcut on my desktop. I *will* revisit this often, I instruct myself, especially since I cannot be consumed with Anthony anymore. He loves someone else. *Ouch*, that stings. But no more distractions. The focus needs to be on Athena.

As I shift my attention to this week's column, I am left thinking about Theo's incredible notebook. He said that his music comes from his experiences, and gives his life meaning. *Meaning.* The very thing that Frankl deduced is the prerequisite for happiness. The plaque at the Jewish Museum also said something about the responsibility to a person you love, *or* to your creative work, as being the 'why' behind your existence. *Hmmm...*

In Theo's case, the commitment to song writing is his 'why.' Why he would do anything that comes his way, including a butt-naked performance, on the road to following his *desire*, his dream. It is his passion. I am a writer as well, so is it also my passion? I always assumed so. I like to write, I am good at it – at least according to my professional accreditations – but I do not write for my own gratification, or for anyone else's for that matter. I write, quite frankly, for a paycheck.

What does that say about me? Do I lack passion? Or have I just not fully discovered it yet? How could I discover it? Maybe my passion is not writing, maybe it is something completely different, but what else do I desire, what else am I willing to commit to – besides a man – that could make my life fulfilled? *What is it going to take to make me happy?*

I am teetering close to the edge of the too many questions not enough answers cliff again. Instead of falling off and losing my way, I take a step back to do, ironically, what is required of me at the moment. To write.

Happiness In a Taxi?

CHAPTER 6

"Finally, I got to name drop and cut the line to get in!" Anthony screams at me over the Reggaeton beat inside Calypso. He managed to find me at the cramped corner I elbowed my way up to at the four-deep stand-alone bar. Inhaling his scent as the thirsty crowd pushes him forward, I fight the urge to feel any type of way about this man. A week's time has healed my irrational feelings of despair over him being in a relationship, but has done little to ease my attraction to him. So, it was a no-brainer that this week's best-of spot had to be a nightclub. A loud, dark, busy nightclub not conducive to seeing or talking to him.

"Glad you're happy!" I yell over my shoulder. "Cranberry with lemon?"

"Yes, please!" He shouts. "I'm sorry if the photos of Theo were a little fuzzy. Without being able to use a flash on that point-and-shoot, I couldn't manipulate the lighting too well. Photoshop helped, I just hope they were usable?"

"Yes, they were fine, don't worry," I shout back. I hand him the small plastic juice cup and take a sip through the straw of my mango mojito. I point to a small clearing behind the bar and we zigzag our way to stand in front of an intricately designed rock wall. Water glides down it like glass, from the ceiling of the clubs third level into the gorgeous bamboo floor beneath our feet. Copper finished steel drums cover the walls that encompass the rest of the circular space, which is lit by rattan lamps hanging from the underside of the two floating tiers.

We turn our backs to the waterfall to observe the sweaty sea of young people grinding on each other. Spread out among them are Afro-Caribbean performers in provocative carnival-style costumes, one of which is gyrating on a rope set ablaze at both ends. Early-twenties Athena would have been in her element here. The drinks are strong, the men's shirts are tight, and the music pumping from the battling deejay's digital turntables is hypnotizing.

Red up-lighting pulses with the bass, and it reminds me of a heartbeat that has given life, rhythm and flow to the thousands of dancing bodies. It is a diverse mix, besides the fact that no one looks a day over thirty. Amazing how all these kids can afford the bottle service in the VIP cabanas high above us. Daddy's credit card, I am guessing.

I hand Anthony my glass to hold as I begin to take notes on the BlackBerry. Anticipating his next question I say, "I'm looking for a student tonight. We have so many subscribers at local colleges; I'd like to give them someone to relate to." I am also hoping that revisiting the stage of life full of newfound freedom and self-expression may help me remember where my passion lies, if I ever had one.

"Makes sense. What about her?" The girl he is alluding to is standing alone about twenty feet away, wearing a tight, shimmery lycra dress. Her fake eyelashes are looking down at the words her long manicured thumbnail is typing into her phone. I nod at Anthony and head over to say hello. She rolls her eyes up at me and squishes her nose.

"Do I know you?"

"I'm Athena Wallace, I write for *The Manhattan Socialite*."

Her face relaxes and she snaps her phone into her pink tinfoil clutch. "I like your magazine. We're actually doing a project on it in one of my classes. I'm Charlene."

"Charlene, it's nice to meet you. This is Anthony –" her eyes assess every inch of him as he waves at her – "and we're here to do a review of this place, as well as a story about a patron. Do you think you could help us out?"

"Maybe. What kind of story?"

"A feature on a college student, how she spends a night out in the city. You said you're doing a class project on *The Socialite*?"

"Yeah, in my magazine production class. I'm a journalism major at Hofstra. I actually intern at NBC Studios, I'm just coming from a late meeting there. Didn't have time to go all the way back home, so my friends are meeting me here."

"Sounds like we have a lot in common, Charlene, and that this might benefit you with your class as well. So, what do you say? Would you like to be in *The Socialite*?"

"Depends. Will there be pictures?"

"Yes."

"Of me?"

"Yes."

"You can get me and my friends in any club without waiting in line?"

"Yes."

"You paying for drinks?" *This heifer has no shame.*

"Sure, but just yours. Not your friends."

"Then my answer is yes." She guzzles the rest of her beverage and shakes the cup at Anthony. "They should be here in a few minutes. Get me another Long Island please?"

"You know I'm a photographer, not a cocktail waitress," he says into my ear, while handing me back my full drink to take her empty one.

"I know, I'm sorry. Put it on my tab, they'll comp it anyway," I reply, then turn to Charlene. "So, you intern at NBC? That's impressive."

"Yeah, I guess. What's his deal?" She watches Anthony walk away like a lioness stalking a gazelle.

"He's the photographer, and taken. He's like thirty-five anyway."

"Oh. Gross. What were you asking? My internship? It's cool. I got to watch Carson Daly do his late show a few weeks ago. He's old too, but still totally hot."

"Totally, but what I meant is, you must be doing well in school to get such a great opportunity. Those connections will be invaluable when you graduate. Trust me, I worked for the *New York Times* one summer in grad school. I took classified ads over the phone, but the fact that the Times was on my resumé was all any employer cared about."

"Um, I have like a 2.0, but I can be really persuasive, especially to my male professors. The program works with NBC and News 12 in Long Island – have you ever seen those anchors? Their stylists must be visually impaired. I had to get the NBC thing if I plan on meeting anyone in the fashion industry."

"Fashion industry?"

"Yeah... Honestly, I don't give a flying fuck about journalism. I didn't have a strong enough portfolio to get into FIT so this is my way around it. If it doesn't work out, there's plenty of wealthy, nerdy execs at the network that are desperate for a young girlfriend to show off."

Unsure how to react, I open my mouth to respond, but nothing comes out.

"I'm kidding. Well, kinda. Wait, can that all be off the record? What are you writing about, again?"

"A little bit about you, what you do for fun, what brought you here tonight."

"Let's start over. I'm from New Rochelle, New York; I love to sew and design dresses for me and my girlfriends to go out in. I actually created the little number I'm wearing right now. If you like it, I could hook you up with something a lil' sexier than what you got on." She sizes me up and down. "What are you, like an eight?" I smile and nod, even though I want to cuss her out. *Girl, I'm a six, I'm just on my period.*

"I'm a junior at Hofstra, I think I already told you that; um, I'm currently single, and came to Calypso to dance with some cute boys."

I ask her a few questions about her opinion of the club, and Anthony returns as Charlene is talking about fist pumping being "sooo three years ago." He hands her the cocktail and I see another girl in a short dress with fake breasts up to her chin, hollering in our direction and juggling three shot cups. At first, I assume it must be one of Charlene's friends. Then she steps under one of the lamps, revealing skin too loose to belong to a twenty-something-year-old.

"Boo! There you are. I've been looking everywhere for you! This place is *so* wack." I look from side to side to see who she could possibly be talking to, and am thoroughly confused when she plants an extremely inappropriate, nauseating kiss on Anthony.

When she removes her tongue from his mouth, he asks, "Hey baby, what are you doing here?"

"I'm out with the girls and dragged them in so I could say a quick 'heyyy.' I know you're working, but I couldn't resist seeing my boo."

Renée turns to me but I am gone before she can get one syllable out. I may have come to terms with the fact that Anthony has a girlfriend, but that does not mean I want to exchange pleasantries with her.

I hide out in the bathroom for a solid ten minutes. *Who the fuck says wack anymore?* I stew over her statement as I alternate between chewing on my mint specked ice cubes and compulsively blotting my lip stain. *As a matter of fact, Calypso's not wack, it happens to be a very hip spot that I, a very well-*

respected columnist, have selected as "best nightclub in the city that you don't need to know someone to get into." I would know because I have been a lot of places. Where has she been? I bet she goes to the generic, over-priced tourist bars in Times Square. Now that's wack. I was worried about her being a model. Pssh. Maybe a 1997 model. Used and dented with a lot of miles. Domestic too. The only accent she's got is in her name. I bet she's ghetto enough not to even spell that right. It's probably something like R-U-N-A-Y. Wait. Did I just say the word "hip" to myself? Jesus, I am getting old.

I reapply the color I have wiped off my lips and focus on my reflection in the mirror. I exhale deeply and let myself for one moment feel disappointment over the reality of Renée. Then I smooth the fly-a-ways on the top of my head and walk out the bathroom door.

I am relieved to find only Charlene and Anthony standing together when I return.

"Athena! Where'd you run off to? I was about to introduce you to my girl – "

I cut him off before he can finish saying the foul word. "Sorry, I thought I saw Chris Brown in one of the cabanas, but it wasn't, and then it took forever to get back down here."

"Well you missed the delicious shots Renée brought us!" Charlene boasts. I notice that she is holding a fresh Long Island Iced Tea.

"You can have mine," Anthony offers. "I told her I didn't want it but she gave it to me anyway."

I hold up my hand to decline.

"I'll take it!" Charlene says.

Anthony hesitates while searching my eyes for a sign that he should not give it to her, but I cannot really say anything, even though I am starting to get nervous that her affinity for alcohol might interfere with my story. He hands it to her and within two seconds the shot is gone.

"Hey Charlene, when are your friends getting here?" I ask.

"I don't know, they should of been here by now." She takes out her phone and shakes her head. "They can't get in. The bouncer wouldn't take their IDs. They want us to meet them at Paulie's."

"Wait. Are you twenty-one?" I ask, my body tensing up. I cannot write about a minor in a bar, let alone one whose drinks are on my tab.

"Yeah, my birthday was last month, but two of my friends aren't yet. Those assholes owe me the thirty dollars I paid to get in here." I breathe a short-lived sigh of relief.

"Well, I guess we have to go to Paulie's then," I say.

Charlene makes an extended trip to the restroom while Anthony and I wait at the coat check.

"What's Paulie's?" He inquires, as the attendant retrieves our jackets.

"It's the underage hangout for college kids. They specialize in Keystone Light and sticky floors."

"Can't wait," he replies sarcastically.

A pungent vanilla body spray precedes her, and Charlene finally arrives to hand over the ticket for her plastic bag filled with work clothes. As I am stuffing a five in the tip jar, Anthony has to catch our off-balance subject by the arm.

"Whoa. You all right?" Even though the music is now muffled background noise, she shouts her response.

"Yeah I'm fine! It's so hot in here! Let's go."

When we get to the sidewalk, I have to call after her. "Charlene! Where are you going? Paulie's is this way!"

"Oh yeah!" she slurs, spinning around and pushing past us. I hope the cold wind sobers her up a little. I know if I had that many drinks in such a short amount of time I would be under the table. Oh yeah... that did happen. I was quite literally under the table.

Our destination is only a few doors down. I am at the front of the line talking to the bouncer, when Anthony's concerned voice calls my name. He is holding Charlene's hair as she is puking over the curb. I rush over to them and pull tissues from my purse to wipe her face.

"Sweetie, you okay? Want me to go inside and find your friends?" I ask. She is very disoriented and is trembling.

"Who? Where is –?" Her eyes are closing and Anthony stops her from falling into the puddle of vomit.

"Your friends, Charlene. Tell me the names of your friends!" I demand.

She is silent and her breathing is staggered and shallow.

"We need to get her to the hospital," Anthony asserts. He sits cross-legged on the sidewalk and lays her barely conscious head in his lap. My hands shake as I dial Taj's number. I have never seen someone this drunk before, and it is scaring the hell out of me. Thank God I anticipated bar hopping tonight, and asked him to be on call. Within minutes, we are in the cab on our way to St. Luke's.

The three of us prop her arms around Anthony and me, and we carry her into the emergency room. The intake nurse rushes over with a wheelchair.

"What happened?" she asks dryly.

"I think it's alcohol poisoning. She had some really strong drinks and a few shots. Here's her ID." I remove Charlene's driver's license from her clutch, as the nurse shines a tiny flashlight into her eyes.

"I can smell that she's had a lot to drink, but this isn't alcohol poisoning. Her pupils are the size of quarters. Honey, what are you on?" Charlene's mumbling is incomprehensible. "Do you know what she took?" she asks Anthony.

"What she took?"

"Ectasy? Cocaine?"

"Oh, um, I'm not sure. We just met her tonight. We didn't see her take anything, but she did spend a long time in the bathroom," he responds.

"Mm hmm. I'll take her from here," the nurse says, waving us off.

"Let me just do one thing, please?" I locate her phone and call the number of the person she last texted, and leave a voicemail letting them know where she is. The nurse then takes Charlene's belongings from me and wheels her through the double doors. We stand in silence for a minute, before Anthony turns to me and sighs.

"We should probably stay until someone gets here," he says.

"Yeah, we probably should."

According to the clock humming in its cage on the waiting room wall, it is nearly three a.m. before four scantily clad college girls stumble in.

"Where's our friend? We want to see our friend!" one of them screeches at the front desk. I flip the ancient issue of *Jet* onto an empty seat as I overhear the admissions clerk calmly explain that Charlene is now a patient in the hospital, so the only visitors allowed are family.

"That's bullshit! We want to see our fucking friend!" another one screams, and then kicks open the double doors that lead to the triage area with an out-of-season cork wedge. "Char, are you in there?"

This gets the attention of the security guard, who is not the least bit amused to have to abandon his newspaper and coffee. While he attempts to deal with the hot messes, I use the pen chain-linked to the counter to write a note on the back of one of my business cards. "Hope you feel better. Please let me know that you're okay."

The clerk assures me she will get it to Charlene.

You may want an energy drink, it's going to be a long night," I say to Anthony, tapping the vending machine as we depart the ER.

"What are you suggesting? By the time we get back to Calypso it's going be last call."

"I'm suggesting the only thing we can do. Get back into the cab. Maybe by some miracle we'll pick up a club-going sober person. A priest who was out booty shaking with nuns, in need of a ride back to the monastery. I don't know. We'll have to fill in the blanks."

"You're funny when you're stressed."

We find Taj in the parking lot Lysol-ing his back seat. "Sorry, Taj. Hope it's not too nasty in there," I say.

"It is okay, miss. I have seen worse. How is she?"

"She was admitted into the hospital, they think she overdosed on drugs."

"Ahh. I cannot understand these American youth. They have everything right in their hand but still see a need to escape from their life." He taps two fingers inside his palm as he speaks.

"I don't know either. I just hope she'll be all right. Meanwhile, I don't have much I can write about. I hate to ask you this, but do you mind if we tag along with you for a bit? In the off-chance you pick up someone interesting for me to write about?"

"I do not mind at all, but you both will have to sit up front with me to make room for passengers. My shift is over in less than two hours, so that does not allow for many possibilities."

"We'll take what we can get," I reply. "Thank you, Taj."

There is not much room on the bench seat so my knees are forced to touch Anthony's. A week ago, this would have felt electric. Now, it is just irritating.

"When I am not driving you, miss, I usually pass by the bars at this time, as people are beginning to leave."

"Perfect. Can we go back to the spot we came from?"

"This is no problem." "You didn't get any photos yet, right?" I ask Anthony. "You can take a few shots of the club from the street."

"I can, but what if we pick up someone coming out of a different bar? You must've been to all of them along that strip. Can't you just adjust your review based on where they've been?"

"No, Calypso's the best... I'm not compromising my column. I'll figure it out."

"Alright, it's your call," he replies skeptically.

One lackluster juice-head bouncer and two inebriated frat boys later, I am no closer to having a face of New York for week four of *Come Here Often*. Alpha and Kappa are passed out in the back seat with their heads together, and I am racking mine for a way to bullshit my way through a story, when someone's cell phone rings. *Let me guess, Renée.* Yet it is Taj who answers his phone. He is speaking in his native tongue, which I have never heard before. It is a short conversation, and when it is over, he explains.

"My wife. She has finished the job a few minutes early. She works the third shift, sorting packages and loading them onto the trucks. Every night she is my last passenger, but this will not be for much longer. She is expecting our first child and they will not allow her to lift anymore. So, if you hear of any place hiring where I am eligible to take a second job, it would be much appreciated."

"A second job? Taj, you work twelve-hour shifts. When would you have time?" I ask.

"It is against the rules of my company to drive all seven days, so I do not work on Mondays. Also, I only require three or four hours of rest in the morning, but my shift does not begin everyday until five p.m. So you see, there is much wasted time, when I could be earning more income."

He turns the steering wheel sharply to the right and slams on the brakes. The two boys heads clunk together but neither stirs. Taj reaches into the backseat and shakes one of them.

"Guys! Guys! This is your stop. Twenty-one fifty please."

They slowly come to, and while one wipes away drool with the back of his hand another fishes in his hoody for the fare. He balls up a twenty and two ones and throws them at Taj.

"Keep the change buddy," he grumbles, and slams the door. *What assholes.* I am sure Taj has to deal with this kind of behavior on a regular basis, and the thought saddens me. He is such a nice man, always so kind to me, and... that is all I really know about him. I have talked to Taj every Saturday night for the past two years, but the only fact about his life that I am unsure of, besides the information he has just shared, is that he drives me where I need to go. *How is that possible?*

"Hey, Taj? Don't feel like you have to say yes to my next question, but if you did, you'd be doing me a really huge favor and the honor of getting to know you better." The degree of my desperation is no secret, thus he knows what I am implying.

"Why would you want to write about me, miss? My life is very boring. Almost every day I drive this cab, pick up my wife from her job, we share a meal, go to bed, then wake to be at home or go to the market before I do this all over again. There is no story there."

"I disagree. Please let me ask you a few questions? It could help you out, too. A lot of important people read our magazine and chances are they'd recognize you at a job interview. I'll even talk to my boss to see if we can put a blurb in highlighting your credentials."

"Credentials?"

"Your good qualities. If anyone has work for you, they can contact me. What do you say? Please?" He rubs the back of his neck and turns his eyes into mine. "Pretty please?" I beg, touching my hands together. Taj clicks off the cab's top center light to signal he is off duty.

"You make it very hard to say no. So I will say, okay. It is a short drive to fetch Tila, so I will not have to talk for long,"

"Thank you for this Taj, sincerely." I am too tired at this hour to start typing, and since it is quiet in the car, I am able to use the voice recorder app on my BlackBerry. "Please state your full name, age, and address. Then you can start by telling me where you're from and what brought you to New York City."

He shifts the cab into drive and leans to speak into my phone. "Hello. I am Taj Prasad Sharma – S-H-A-R-M-A – of 5224 Roosevelt Drive, Queens, New York, apartment number five B. I am twenty-eight years, and originally from the country of Bhutan."

I always thought by the way he carries himself that he was older than me. I also assumed he was Indian, like many of the other cab drivers in the city. *Ignorant, Athena.*

"If you have never heard of it, Bhutan is a very small country, near to India on one side and China on the other. I do not have much memory of what it is like there. I went to live in Beldangi II camp in Nepal many years ago, when I was just six years old. My wife Tila and I were very lucky to come to the United States in the month of August in 2009. We were resettled in a place called Utica where we stayed for a short time, until we learned that Tila had a cousin living in Queens. So this is why we moved to New York City, to be with family."

"I didn't know you were a refugee, Taj," I say. "Can you tell me more about that? What was it like living in a camp?"

"It was very crowded in the beginning. Nine of us lived together in a hut about as big as three taxicabs. There was myself, my auntie, three brothers and four sisters. We had a fire to cook food, and only mats to sleep on the dirt floor. Toilets had not yet been built; we had to use the forest for this purpose. We spent most days playing outside and going to the school, so as children it did not seem so terrible, but I was very sad most of the time, missing my parents."

"Where were they?" I ask.

"My father was killed by the Royal Army while marching for equal rights for the Lhotshampa people. You see, our ancestors came to Bhutan from Nepal maybe one hundred years before. The problems began when the government decided Nepali people were no longer welcome. That we were a threat to the culture of Bhutan. My mother wanted to keep us there after my father died, to honor what he believed in, but it became very dangerous.

"The school in our village was bombed, and we had to stay inside all day. One day, a group of men broke into our home, and they saw my father's picture on our wall. They became very mad because behind him in that picture was the flag of the Bhutan Peoples' Party. Their opposition."

Taj's face hardens and his tone softens. "They spoke terribly to my mother, and kicked her and beat her. They raped her in front of all her children until she was dead. I remember sitting next to her body, holding her hand and crying for many hours. I watched my sister Sumitra be silent, rocking the two infants, until my auntie came to get us. We had to leave right away, in case of the men's return, and were each allowed to carry one thing with us from our home.

"My older sisters, they took their favorite clothing, but I would not leave my mother's side to choose something. My auntie was very upset with me, that I would not go. She tells me this story, that she showed me each of my toys and I told her no! Finally, I pointed to the picture of my father. That is the only thing I have now from my home. The only memory of my father."

I do not know what to say to Taj, as a tear runs down my cheek. I feel Anthony's leg stiffen, and remember the story of the photo album with his mother's pictures.

"Please do not cry for me, miss. I was just a baby. My life now is good, I am very lucky."

"What about your siblings?" Anthony asks.

"The oldest one is Krishna, he still lives in the camp. He took it very, very hard. He does not speak much and is given many medicines to help him with his nightmares. Sumitra is also there with her husband and children. They were told they would be coming to the US for three years now, but they have not yet received their interviews.

"From what I know, two of my sisters are in the Netherlands, and the youngest, Hari, is in England. She is the one that never met our father, because my mother, she was pregnant with her when he was killed. My other two brothers and their families are in Quebec City, in Canada. Tila and I have been saving our money so that we can take a trip there. It is unusual that we have not been placed together, and makes me very upset for my family to be apart like this. Tila has only one sister, who is caring for her ailing parents in the camp. I do not think they will ever be able to come here, but we pray that they do."

"I will pray for this, too. I'm sorry Taj, I didn't know it's been so hard for you. We can stop this if you want," I say.

"No, I do not mind talking to you; well, talking to everyone in Manhattan, I suppose. Your help in finding a second job is very important to me. It is difficult to search without my own car."

"I promise you, I'll do my absolute best to make that happen."

"I thank you for that. I can finish speaking of my life in the refugee camp, if you'd like?"

"Please."

"My auntie, she never took a husband because she was too busy caring for her sister's children. She remains there also, watching over Krishna. I send her letters and money whenever I am able to, and have just heard from her on the phone only a few days ago during Dashain. That is our best Nepali festival, when we celebrate the family being reunited. There are many rituals happening in the camp. I miss these..."Taj closes his eyes for a moment, then shakes his head. "You know, my life was not bad there. I was very busy and had many friends. You may not believe me, but I worked shortly as an engineer's apprentice in India. My studies prepared me for this, and I was able to leave the camp for four months to do such work. The refugees are not allowed to stay in that country, so I returned, also to marry Tila.

"After this time, I worked as a leader in the camps, educating the Nepali on our history. Neighboring camps asked me to come and speak to their people, too. My father, he would have been proud of me for this work – I believe it is the reason I was chosen to come here. My caste, my family name, is very respected in Nepal. Maybe not so much in New York," he sighs.

"I was very fortunate to go to college in Nepal. This means nothing in America. My teacher since grade one helped me to become matriculated. He believed in me very much. Like another father, making certain I focused on my studies and stayed out of trouble. This must not have been an easy task. I was a very curious child, always meddling in the adult's business.

"He used to say to me 'Char, you are a very intelligent boy, with eyes and ears as big as the elephant's. Please be at peace with the evil you have seen and heard, and allow your heart to grow to their size. Then you will have the ability to do anything you wish.' If you are curious as to why he called me by this name, Char, it is because it is Nepali for the number four. My siblings are very close in age, so there were many of us together in the school. Our teachers liked to call us by the number of our birth, for fun. I was my mother's fourth child.

"I am sorry to think my teacher would be sad to see my work now, driving around the engineers. Money is so important in America, more important than the job. This is not to complain. It is a blessing to be here. I have just heard this word, 'blessing,' from a man I was driving tonight. Am I using it correctly?" I assure him that he is. "Then it really is a blessing to be here. With good health, a nice home with my wife, and in my cab with you." He smiles kindly at us.

"You are a remarkable man, Taj. We are the ones blessed to know you." The leather seat crinkles as Anthony leans across me to squeeze his shoulder.

"Yes, Taj. I can't thank you enough for allowing me to share your story. When is your baby due?" I ask.

"In three months, January. We are excited to have our son with us. We are naming him Mani, in honor of my father." He lifts his hips to get the wallet from his back pocket, and unfolds a paper from inside of it. I am choked up all over again when he hands me the tattered photograph. Many tears have fallen within the last few weeks – over my ruined skirt, and Anthony's relationship – but until now they have not been shed over anything of meaning.

"He looks very strong, very handsome. Like you. Would it be all right if Anthony took a picture of your picture?"

"It is all right. Now, here is my wife." I had not noticed that we had pulled up to the front gate of a massive UPS facility.

Anthony rolls down his window and Tila shouts something at Taj. They have a brief exchange, during which the only word I pick up on is 'credentials.' Tila's mood appears to shift and she approaches.

"Her English is not so good. I have told her you are with me to write about me in your magazine. That you will help us to make more money. She is happy about that."

"Taj, women are the same in every language. Let me snap a photo of the two of you outside the cab before we go," Anthony says.

Taj gets out to stand with Tila. They pose, but do not smile.

"Sir, if you are able, may I please have one of these photos to send my family in Nepal? I think it will bring them much happiness to see us."

"You can have as many as you want. I will make sure Athena gets them to you."

Taj shakes Anthony's hand. I am pleased that we are able to help him, and that our night has come to a positive end.

At 5:32 a.m., I finally arrive home. Today has been mentally exhausting. I am so tired I do not even bother to brush my teeth or pick my clothes off the floor before crawling into bed. God knows the last time I prayed over something that was not clothing related has been too long, but before I lay down I am overcome with the need to bow my head. I ask the universe to bless Taj, Tila, and their unborn child, and to reunite their family very soon. I pray for Charlene, that she is recovering, and if she suffers from addiction, that she is motivated to seek treatment.

I also express my gratitude for being born in a safe place, for having my parents and my friends nearby, for my job and The only loss I have endured is the passing of my grandmother, who was old and went peacefully in her sleep. It was difficult for me, but hardly comparable to watching your mother being raped and beaten to death. Yet for all he has been through, Taj was reluctant to complain about anything in his life, for fear it might make him seem ungrateful. Meanwhile, I am swimming in an abyss of apathy and self-loathing, and have known nothing of tragedy or suffering in my life. I need to start acting more grateful for that.

This overwhelming sense of humbleness does not leave me overnight, and the first thing I do when I wake is return my mother's call from a week ago. While she is rambling on and on about setting me up with a veterinarian who is recently divorced with two adorable kids and a perfectly fine choice because, you know, I am at that age where I am just going to have to accept the fact that the available men come with baggage, my mind does its usual wandering.

However, the frustration from which this wandering typically springs has been replaced today with appreciation. Yes, my mother is an insufferable broken record sometimes, but I am lucky to have her love and concern in my life. I pretend to write down Dr. Doolittle's phone number, and tell her that I love her very much before hanging up.

The coffeepot has finished brewing, and it is a toss-up whether to spend the afternoon soul searching or watching the *Ice Loves Coco* marathon. I compromise and put the TV on mute, but since inspiration tends to hide from me in the quiet, I also use the remote to switch on the iPod. Amaretto creamer along with the sounds of Maxwell warm my neo soul.

I access iCloud on my laptop and open *My Reflections*. Under where I left off last time (had fun until... girlfriend... depression) I relay my thoughts on this week's assignment.

Week 4 - "Char"
<u>Charlene escaped her reality by choice, Taj escaped his by force</u>
Importance of and dedication to family/friends
Overcome tragedy, "blessing to be here"
GRATITUDE

At this point, I turn off "Fistful of Tears" to play back yesterday's interview on my BlackBerry. I add, "Allow your heart to grow" before closing the MacBook. Sprawled out with a chenille throw, I zone out on the closed captioning for a prescription pimple cream commercial, then take to picking at the buttons on the back of the sofa.

It is really bothering me that I never thought to ask Taj about himself before. Besides my close friends, around whom I have already resolved to behave less Athena-centrically, am I only concerned with others in regard to what they contribute to my life? Am I really that shallow and selfish of a person? Deep down I know the answer is no, but my behavior to the contrary makes me uneasy. On this new journey of self-discovery, I have to work on being more aware of not only myself, but of the world around me.

I cannot really explain it, but after hearing Taj's story last night, a part of me changed. The images his words painted will forever be ingrained in my head, and the feelings evoked by them, in my heart.

*****

"What are you doing here first thing on a Monday?" I am surprised to see Anthony sitting at his desk on the way to my office.

"Good morning to you too, Athena. Brian called while I was on my way to a shoot and asked me to come in right away. Here, take a look at this."

I step into his cubicle to peer over his shoulder at the computer screen. Setting my coffee cup down, I find it curious that a photographer does not have a single framed photo of a loved one on his desk. That would have spared me a whole lot of grief. Well, if I am being honest, probably not.

"Pictures from Saturday night?" I ask, as he zooms out on a photo he has been editing.

"Yes, I'm printing this one for you to give Taj." The sight of a stoic Taj with his arm around Tila and the checkered cab artfully blurred in the background brings a smile to my face.

Anthony dashes to the copy room around the corner, just as Brian appears in the hallway.

"Hi Brian, how was your weekend?" I ask, but do not give him a chance to respond. "I wanted to talk to you about my column this week. It's not about a person at a nightclub, but the man who *brings* you to the club; my cab driver, Taj. You're going to be blown away by his story. He's an incredible person, a refugee, and his wife is about to have a baby and lose her job, so he could really use our help finding more work. I was hoping you wouldn't mind if I wrote a line or two regarding this?"

"Sure, Athena, but keep it brief. Your column isn't the classified section. You, in my office, now," Brian barks at Anthony.

I am handed two copies of the photo and shot a confused glance before he follows Brian down to his office. The door slams and I can feel glittery shadowed eyes burning a hole in the back of my head.

"I thought I told you to tone down the makeup."

Mark flicks his wrist at me. "It's hardly noticeable. What was *that* about?"

"I have no idea. I've never seen Brian like that before."

"Come on." Mark grabs my arm and we have a tug of war with it before he wins and drags me to the closed door.

"You're really strong for a girl," I complain under my breath, rubbing my elbow. He puts his ear up to the door and I crouch behind him.

"Nothing to see here, move along, move along," Mark snaps at Larry, the fashion writer, as he strolls by.

"What are they saying?" I whisper. Mark shushes me and holds up one finger.

"If I find out that you... something about compromising the integrity of the magazine... something about never working in this industry again... something about now get the fuck out of my office... *Shit!*" He takes my hand and pulls me into my office. Five seconds later Anthony darts past.

"What'd he do?" Mark asks.

I shrug and roll my desk chair to the doorway. I peek both ways down the empty corridor, before rolling next to Mark and responding, "Whatever it was, it must have been serious. I think he left."

Mark clutches his chest when the sound of Brian's voice thunders through the intercom. "Athena, Anthony won't be working with you for the time being. Freelance Freddie can go with you on your next assignment. I suggest you contact him and make arrangements."

"But why –?"

"If you don't have Freddie's number, get it from Mark." The intercom clicks off.

"Ugh, Freelance Freddie. Or 'almost dead Fred,' as I like to call him. You've been seriously downgraded, honey," Mark bemoans.

"I know," I say, frowning, even though a part of me knows the change is probably a good thing. "Can you please get me that number? Try to get to the bottom of this Anthony thing, too."

"Oh, rest assured, I'm on it." Mark turns to leave, but bumps into a uniformed man holding a box covered with tissue paper.

"Oops, sorry about that, um, *sir.*" He does a double take at Mark. "I'm looking for Athena Wallace? There's no one at the front desk so I came on back."

"I'm Athena..."

"Rockefeller Florist ma'am. I have a delivery for you." Mark claps and jumps up and down as I accept the package and send the courier on his way.

"Who's it from? Who's it *from*?" he squeals with delight.

"I don't know, back up off me!" I nudge him off my neck and he squeals again.

"What's the card say? What's it *say*?"

"Athena, can't wait to read my article. Thank you again for the publicity. Here's my contact info as requested. 1029 North Tremont Street, blah blah blah. Hope you enjoy the plant. Theo."

I tear open the paper to unveil a tall, suggestive looking cactus, surrounded by two shorter, round cacti. Mark looks at it sideways and I giggle.

"Who's Theo? And why did he send you a dick plant?"

"Read my column this week and you'll find out. Right now I have some serious blogging to do, so can you please return to your reception quarters and get me old man river's – "

"– almost dead Fred."

"–almost dead Fred's number?" I shove Mark towards the door but he digs his stacked heels in, still staring at the cactus. "What, do you want to borrow it?"

"No! I'm not into getting pricked by a prick. But hey, it gives whole new meaning to the word succulent, doesn't it?" He licks his lips and I purse my own.

"Go, already with your foul self!" With one more hard thrust, Mark prances away.

*****

Wednesday comes, and a disk of photos has been placed on my desk, but no sign of the person who left it. By Friday, Anthony still has not made an appearance or returned my phone calls. Also, I am a little worried because I have not heard from Charlene, either. When I called the hospital they told me she had been released, but would not disclose any other details. Maybe my card never got to her. Or maybe she could not care less about me, now that there is not going to be a glossy picture of her and her poom-poom dress in a magazine.

As I am shutting everything down for the weekend, I decide to get a head start on Monday's rituals and tear three days off the quote-a-day calendar. I toss out today and Sunday's, but tuck Saturday's in the plastic pick that held Theo's note in the plant and contemplate it.

There is no passion to be found in settling for a life that is less than the one you are capable of living. ~ Nelson Mandela

Week four began miserably, with a search for misplaced passion, but ended up bitch slapping me out of my funk and teaching me more important lessons about gratitude and awareness. I have been shaken back to reality, with renewed energy and the realization that I have to stop taking myself so seriously. Though I do have to take making myself happy seriously, this must be done, at least in part, by living more consciously.

As far as my passion goes, I am sure I was over-thinking this before. Of course it is writing. I do not know why I doubted that, because it always has been. I used to bring my trapper-keeper to my grandma's house after school, and we would sit at her kitchen table together eating generic Nilla Wafers and writing sultry romance novels, like her collection of Danielle Steel's.

Sultry, to an eight-year-old, being a tongue kiss by a boy behind a tree in the park. Over time though, they evolved into quite the collection of short stories, and I was going to become a rich and famous author.

I was going to buy my grandma a house in Beverly Hills with a swimming pool and a maid. She always encouraged my creativity, and I loved spending that time with her. Until I got too busy writing term papers to write for fun anymore. Just because I make a living at it now, albeit in a different way than I had dreamed, that does not make writing any less meaningful to me.

If anything, this assignment has brought me closer to finding meaning than anything else I have ever done. I feel like I am on the verge, that the dawn to my darkness is breaking. No matter what the last two weeks of this assignment bring, I promise myself I will not give up until I am standing in the light.

Happiness In Cancer?

CHAPTER 7

"This means very much to me, thank you." Taj pulls out the glossy photographs from the envelope I have handed over the front seat of the cab.

"You're very welcome, and I have exciting news! My boss was so moved by your story that he showed it to his boss right away, who wants to offer you a job driving one of our delivery trucks. It would be part-time of course, around your work schedule, and you wouldn't be making tips, but I hear the pay is pretty decent. What do you think? I wrote his name and phone number down for you, it's attached to one of the photos. He said he'd understand if you want to wait and see if my column generates any better offers, but I'd reach out to him soon if you're interested."

Taj removes the purple post-it from underneath the paperclip and holds it under the dome light to decipher my penmanship.

"No need to wait, I will call him Monday morning. This is a wonderful thing you have done. I do not know what Tila and I can do to repay you."

"You've already done more than enough, really. How is Tila feeling, anyway?"

"She is well, but starting to have some back pain. She is finished with the job next Friday, so this news has come at the best time for us."

"I'm glad. Oh, and I'll bring a copy of *The Socialite* with me next week so you can see the piece I've written. I hope you like it."

"I am not concerned with liking it. I am only happy to help you with your job, as you have done for me. Will I also be able to thank the photographer for these pictures?"

"He won't be joining me tonight, but I'll pass on your thanks the next time I see him." *Whenever that may be.* We sit in silence for a moment, before Taj stuffs the paper back into the envelope and turns the ignition.

"Please excuse me, miss! You have made me so happy, I have forgotten about my current job!"

"It's okay, Taj, you know that I like being fashionably late. I'm going to The Shack please, on Ninth Ave in Midtown West. Nice Halloween costume, by the way." I am referring to his giant statue of liberty hat and the red, white, and blue beaded necklaces that have been clacking together during our exchange.

"A gift from my friend, Ram, who sells such things from his cart. He told me the Americans will be dressing for the holiday this weekend, so I should too. I like what you are wearing also, very beautiful. Who is the person you are dressed as?"

"Athena, the Greek goddess." The back of his head nods.

"Would you mind turning the radio to 105.1? It looks like we might be stuck in traffic for a bit."

I am singing along to Miguel's "Adorn" when we reach the biker bar, where almost dead Fred is standing conspicuously under the old-fashioned blinking arrow sign out front, using an obnoxiously giant camera to photograph the rows of parked motorcycles. The man is probably only in his early sixties, as Mark does have a tendency to exaggerate; however, the fact that his pleated, khaki pants fall inches above his ankle, exposing white tube socks snuggly tucked into brown loafers, does not exactly give him the appearance of a spring chicken.

I resist the urge to ask if he has film in his camera as I greet him. "Hey Freddie, sorry if I kept you waiting. We hit a lot of detours. I think they shut down some streets around Central Park for the haunted carriage rides. Where's your Halloween costume?"

"I figured I didn't have to wear anything special to a place called The Shack. You mean to tell me this face isn't scary enough?" He snickers at his own joke.

"No, it's not scary at all, but you need something to blend a little more..." I take off my gold leaf crown and place it atop his apricot colored comb-over. "If anyone asks, you're Zeus, and that big flash is your lightning bolt."

He hangs the camera around his neck and follows me inside. It is a relatively small space, almost every inch of which is decorated with patrons' graffiti and pictures from the bar's signature contests. Under a sky of license plates, burly bikers in Harley Davidson shirts drink canned beer alongside Wall Street bikers wearing suits and sipping white wine. About half of them are actually wearing some type of Halloween flair. My favorite has to be the tattooed fairy princess, who is using a butterfly wand to scratch his ZZ Top beard.

We find two empty bar stools beneath a motorcycle headlight, and I take a seat on my prized YSL leather jacket – a diamond in the clearance rack rough.

"What're you drinking, Freddie?"

"I'll have what you're having," he responds.

Behind the bar there is a familiar face sporting a hot pink and brown leopard mohawk. She sets two cocktail napkins down and leans over the sticky surface for a hug.

"Athena, how are you? Back so soon?"

"Hey, Ashley! I'm so glad you're working tonight. I know, I just did a review over the summer, but I love this place so much I'm writing about it again as best biker bar in Manhattan."

"That's awesome! Go us! What do you need from me?" Ashley asks.

"Nothing. I brought my man Freddie tonight to take pictures." He flashes a Cheshire Cat smile. "Ashley helped me out last time by emailing some photos from their famous contests. You're going to school for photography, right?"

"That's right, you remember. I'm coming up on the end of my last semester. I actually just got a callback for a second interview at a major modeling agency. Keeping my fingers crossed that I can finally leave this dump."

"Hey, Miley Cyrus, you gonna talk or get me a beer?" She gives the guy three stools down the finger without turning away from us.

"I'm kidding, I love it here too. How could I not? Now what can I get 'cha?"

"Two house drafts, please," I say.

"I like your costume, Athena. You should enter the contest tonight," Ashley suggests as she pours our beers.

"Oh yeah? Last time I was here it was 'who can spin the longest on a bar stool before falling off while wearing ass-less chaps and playing the harmonica.' I'm definitely not that coordinated. I would've been the first to face plant with my business all up in the air. What's this one?"

"Another Shack original. Halloween costume meets wet t-shirt," she replies. I laugh and take the overflowing pint from her.

"Thank you, but I think I'll sit this one out, too."

Ashley shrugs and sets down Freddie's beer. "On the house, of course," she says, then goes to wait on the customer six stools down.

Someone turns up the music that is playing in the background. It is blues, and reminds me of Anthony. I cannot help but long for his company when a foam mustached Freddie raves, "Mmm, this is tasty."

"I agree, and I'm not much of a beer drinker," I say. "They brew it themselves. This place used to be a bike shop, and the owner made beer in the back room for his customers. Even grew his own hops in the overgrown lot behind the building. The city caught wind of it and threatened to shut him down, so he had to choose between bikes and beer. This was his compromise."

Freddie looks around and nods. He takes another sip and the 'stache grows thicker. "I did my homework and read your last three columns. Good stuff. So, how does this work? How do you choose who to write about?"

"Depends. The night has a tendency to go its own way, but sometimes I start with a general idea of who to approach. For instance, this week, I'd like to feature a woman. The last four – well, three and a half –" I am referring to the Wild Horses article, "have been about men. Why don't you poke around, take a few photos of the bar, and we'll see who we can come up with."

"Alrighty then." Freddie hops off his stool and takes his beer on the mission with him. I concentrate on taking my usual notes, until Ashley's voice replaces the music through the speakers.

"Hey there guys and girls, it's time for The Shack's Halloween costume contest! Now, you know we like to do things a little different around here, so if you turn your attention to the center of the bar, you'll see that we've hand selected five sexy contestants, each donning a Shack t-shirt over his or her costume. When you all countdown from three, my fellow bartenders will hose them down, and they'll strike their best pose as the person they're dressed as. The contestant who gets the most applause at the end gets to keep the shirt, and drinks for free with a friend all night long. Is everyone ready?" There is a lot of who-hoo'ing and someone whistles loudly.

"Begin the countdown!" Ashley puts down the microphone and picks up her camera.

"Three... two ...one!" Soda guns spray water across the hairy chest of a beer bellied playboy bunny, the bearded fairy princess, a large-breasted Daisy Duke, an equally well endowed black cat, and a flat-chested Wonder Woman with a silver-haired buzz cut. I overhear the guy next to me ask his companion if one of them is famous, as Freddie knocks people out of the way, including Ashley, with his paparazzi worthy lens. I shake my head. At least we will have good pictures.

The two men are hamming it up and the younger girls look like they are auditioning for an eighties rock video, but it is the eldest contestant, sticking her butt and arms straight out, pretending to fly, who wins the audience's vote by a landslide. After receiving hugs from the competition, Wonder Woman is lifted under her arms by the bunny and set on the ground. I abandon my post to join her as she claims her backpack and victory Shirley Temple from the bartender.

"Congratulations! You are a braver woman than me."

"Well thanks, darlin'," she replies sweetly, as she pats herself dry with a bar towel. "But shoot me straight. You sure I didn't look like a crazy old lady up there? I think I may have gotten the sympathy vote," she whispers, shielding her mouth towards me.

"Girl, classy *always* wins over Cancun."

"I like you. Can I get you a drink? It's part of the prize, but Wonder Woman's flying solo tonight."

"No thanks, my drink's complimentary too. I'm doing a review for *The Manhattan Socialite*, my name's Athena."

"Pleasure to meet you. I'm Olivia, but my friends call me Liv."

We shake hands, and the same jackass who harassed Ashley leans in and mutters, "I'll be your friend, Liv."

"Sorry, position's been filled." She turns her back to him and pops a maraschino cherry that she has fished out of the winner's chalice into her mouth. The guy in front of me rises and taps a pack of cigarettes on his palm. I slide into the empty seat.

"So, Athena, how many stars are you giving The Shack?" Liv asks.

"Well, I'm writing that they're the best biker bar in the city, so I guess that would be five. Do you come here often, Liv?"

"Almost every Saturday since I bought my hog in the spring. I suppose that makes me a regular, imagine that! Aren't their contests a hoot?" I agree. "I can't believe I entered one, and won! Oh, if only my kids were here, they'd be so embarrassed... I had Ashley take a picture with my cell, I want to send it to my daughter, but I'll be darned if I know how to use this thing. You think you can help me out? I think I'm the only old lady around who still uses a Blackberry."

I laugh and show her my matching phone. "Of course I can help, us old ladies have to stick together! What's your daughter's name?"

"Aisha. You can send it to my son, too. Solomon." I find them in her contacts and text the picture. "You have a lovely name, by the way. Are you Greek, goddess?"

"My mother is," I answer.

"Such a fascinating culture. Was she born in Greece?"

"Yes, she came here when she was eight. Most of her family still lives there, and both of her parents passed away before I was born, so I wasn't exposed to the culture very much growing up."

"Have you ever been there before? To Greece?"

"No, she hasn't been back, either, but I'd love to go someday."

"And your father, what's his ethnicity?" *Geesh. Who's the reporter here, anyway?*

"He's African-American."

"Well, you are a very unique and lovely combination of the two... and if you are wonderin' why I am being so nosy, part of it is my Southerness comin' out, and the other part is because I am intrigued with ethnic heritage. I actually helped lay the foundation for the 'Black to Africa' study at NYU. Have you heard of it? The study uses DNA samplin' to trace a person's ancestry back to a region, and sometimes even to a specific tribe, in Africa. For example, much of my lineage is shared with the Mozabite people of Algeria. It explains my sharp features and light complexion."

"It's funny that you say that! My dad actually participated, and found out that his genes are predominantly Nubian. I read the handout they gave him, but never took it any further than that. I've been meaning to do more research though... Are you a professor at NYU?"

"Yes, in the anthropology department. Have been since I graduated from there more years ago than I'd like to admit. You'd have found my African civilizations class interestin'. A piece of the curriculum was dedicated to the contributions of the Nubian people to Ancient Egypt. Unfortunately, it's not offered anymore. I'm only teaching one linguistics class now, as an adjunct."

"Why's that?" I ask. She seems too passionate to be pursuing retirement.

"Chemo. My treatment schedule became too hard to work a full class load around. Plus, some days the pain's so bad I can't get out of bed," Liv says nonchalantly.

"Cancer?" I ask, twisting my face from the ugliness of the word.

"Breast cancer, stage four. But I still have hope, darlin' . You've got to! My name's Liv for goodness sakes! You can't ignore that irony, and if I didn't have some type of faith, I'd be numbin' myself with a tall glass of that right now. It was my husband's drink of choice."

She gestures to the Wild Turkey bottle a bartender is using to pour shots. "They say alcohol interferes with the effectiveness of my meds, but who knows what they know? They gave me six months to live, seven months ago. Oh, that reminds me..." She unzips the front pocket of her backpack, retrieves a wrinkled piece of college ruled notebook paper, and smooths it out on the bar. "Can you hand me one of those pencils, darlin'?"

I stretch to pluck a golf pencil from the plastic keno card holder. Liv takes it and draws a line through something on her page.

"What's that you're working on?" I ask.

"You ever heard of a bucket list?"

"Yes."

"Well, this is my fuck it list."

My last sip of beer comes out of my nose at the sound of her dainty voice saying 'fuck.'

"What's that?" I ask after clearing my throat.

"It's the same thing; I just like the name better. You know, my husband Clyde died suddenly of a heart attack when he was only forty-five years old. We were so busy workin' and savin' for retirement, we never took time out to travel together or do the things that really mattered. Those things we said we'd get to once the kids were out of the house and we had enough money in the bank. Then one day I woke up and I was a widow, just like that."

She snaps her fingers. "And you know, you think it would have hit me then how precious every single moment is. That I would have done the things we dreamed about, but I didn't. I just hung my head and went about my business. For twenty whole years. That is, until the day I was diagnosed with an aggressive form of cancer.

"Funny what facing your own mortality will do to you. I think a lot of people simply give up, focus on makin' their final arrangements because in a way it's almost easier... Well, that day I visited Clyde to tell him my prognosis, and prayed over his grave for hours. That's when the idea came to me to start this list. Now, contrary to my behavior this evenin, I've always been the reserved type, from some good Christian stock, but my husband, he was more of a free spirit. Smoked cigars, gambled, drank rye... He's up there laughin' that I call it my fuck it list, and when it's all over, after I take my last breath, we can laugh together."

I smile and gently squeeze her shoulder. "What kind of stuff's on it?"

"Oh, there's your standard dyin' wishes like sky divin' and a trip to Fiji, with a few silly things in between. I've been makin'' it up as I go along. Always carry it with me, and if somethin' peaks my interest, no matter how crazy or unlikely, I write it down. There's also a few fears on there I'm attemptin' to conquer before I leave this earth. Ridin' a motorcycle was the first. It's been a very empowerin' task."

"I think I understand what you mean. My dad's a retired cop, and ever since I was little I was terrified of his gun. So, on my eighteenth birthday, he brought me to a shooting range to fire one. My hands were shaking so bad, but the moment I pulled that trigger I wasn't scared any more. Now I'll even go to the range by myself on occasion, although I haven't been in awhile. It's phenomenal stress relief."

"I like that. I'm goin' to use it. Number ninety-three. Fire. A. Gun." She flips the page over and writes it down.

"Would you mind if I take a look at it?" I ask, tilting my chin at her paper.

"I don't mind at all, darlin'." Liv slides the list over to me, and I am careful not to get beer on it. I see that roughly a third of the items have been crossed off, including number seven. "Participate in a Wet T-shirt Contest."

She must see what I am looking at because she says, "I added that one after havin' my double mastectomy. Never thought the opportunity would actually present itself, but here I am."

I suppress a smile when I notice the next item on her list.
"Liv, I can help you cross off one of the silly things, if you'd like."
"And which one is that?"
"It's a surprise, but you'd have to come back to my loft with me." She does not hesitate to take me up on it.
"Only if you don't mind ridin' my Harley there."
"Are you kidding? I would love to!"

Freddie must have been lingering at a distance, because he joins us when I stand to put my jacket on.

"Hey, Athena, looks like you found the star of the next installment of *Come Here Often*. I got some great shots of her during the costume contest. Let me snap a few more before you go." He raises his camera, but I put my hand over the lens and push it back down, then turn to a confused Liv.

"Oh my God, I am *really* sorry. I was so caught up in our conversation that I completely forgot my purpose for being here tonight. Please believe me. My review is also supposed to tell the story of a person at The Shack. I mean, you would be an incredible choice, but I totally, totally, understand if you say no. That wasn't my intent. I'll find someone else and then you can take me up on my other offer tomorrow, or another day. Whatever works for you."

"Athena, it's okay," she replies kindly. "It would be an honor to be in your column. Lucky for you, there's number fifteen on my list." I scroll down until I read "Have my 15 Minutes of Fame."

"I was sort of hopin' to become famous for my groundbreakin' research in African tribal linguistics, but I think that ship may have sailed. Just promise me that you will write out of interest, and not pity. I don't want anyone feelin' sorry for me. Lucky for me, I've managed to keep most of my hair so I'll still look good in the pictures." She cups her chin in her hand and vogues for the camera.

"Liv's offered me a lift home, Freddie. Can I call you a cab?" I ask as he photographs her.

"No thanks, I think I can find my way home... and that should do it. I'll get these to you A-SAP. Athena, Wonder Woman, it's been real." He bows, and as soon as he turns to leave, I embrace her.

I do not let go for a few seconds, and when I do I take both of her hands in mine and say, "I promise you I will not write out of pity, only inspiration."

"I appreciate that, darlin'. Do you know what etymology is?"

I shake my head.

"It's a part of my field, and a personal interest of mine. It's the study of the history behind words, what they mean. For example, my daughter Aisha's name means 'life.' She was my first-born, that's why I chose it. Your name refers to the goddess of wisdom. My name, Olivia, stems from the Latin word for 'olive tree.' I believe that God brought us together tonight; you, to impart wisdom by tellin' my story, and for the two items you are helpin' to cross off my list.

"And me, well, if you're familiar with your Greek mythology, you'll recall that the olive tree was a gift from Athena to the citizens of Athens. It brought an end to her war with Poseidon, and became a symbol of peace and triumph. Maybe my story can bring peace to someone else out there who's facing their own mortality, whether physically or spiritually. Inspire them to develop a list, to treat each day as an irreplaceable opportunity, and live it accordingly. Or maybe I'm givin' myself a wee bit too much credit." She chuckles.

"But there you go. Etymology. Now enough of my anthropology lecture. I see that the photographer has left with your crown, a thing that a proper Greek goddess should not be without." She places her Wonder Woman crown on my head, then winks and says, "Let me just go dry off a little better under the hand dryer in the bathroom before we go. Wouldn't want to catch a cold out there."

I have just finished informing Taj that I will not be needing a ride home, when Liv joins me where the motorcycles line up on the sidewalk. It is instantly apparent which one belongs to her – a custom Harley, adorned with pink awareness ribbons and a "Liv4evr" license plate. There is a GPS attached to the dash where she has me input my address.

"Ready, darlin'?" She hands me her backpack, and I stuff my purse inside of it before putting my arms through the straps. I lift my white chiffon toga dress, wrap it around my thighs, and swing the gold gladiator sandal that is laced up my calf around to straddle the bike. Liv starts the engine and hands me the pink helmet.

"Here, you wear it," she shouts over the roar of the motor turning over. It fits snugly over my crown. We roll off the curb – Liv carefully manipulating the handlebars, me reflecting on the direction this evening has taken. When I decided on a biker bar for week five, I knew the person I would find would be unconventional, but never could I have imagined I would be riding bitch on a pink Harley behind a sixty-five-year-old woman dressed as a superhero.

I hold on tightly to Liv's slender frame as we weave through the city. The GPS recalculates like mad when we attempt to bypass the congested Central Park area, and I am grateful that the ride takes longer than it should. This is the first time I have been on a motorcycle, so not only do I feel like I am fulfilling my jacket's birthright, but the experience makes me feel incredibly alive.

Our max speed cannot be more than twenty-five miles per hour, but the wind whipping against my exposed skin and through the hair that falls down my back is invigorating. Manhattan looks different from here – smells different – sounds different. In this moment, it is just me and Liv against the world, two powerful women on a crusade to take back our lives. From this angle, age does not exist, nor time, nor limitations. We own this night, but nothing can own us.

When we arrive at the loft, I ask her if she would like a cup of coffee. She accepts, so I turn on the coffeepot and offer her a glass of water in the meantime. I patiently wait for her to take a few sips before declaring, "Now that the formalities are out of the way, close your eyes." I set her glass down on the breakfast bar, take her by the hand, and lead her to my bedroom. Once we are in the walk-in closet, I tug the light bulb string. It takes a minute to find what I am looking for, and when I do, I hold the hanger out in front of her. "I'm ready. You can look now."

She opens her eyes and tilts her head. She runs her fingers down the delicate fabric of the dress. "Is this...?"

"Number eight. Buy a black Givency dress. But I hope it's okay to bend the rules a little, because I'm giving it to you." Liv takes the dress from me and holds it against her.

"Oh, Athena, I can't believe this! It's just gorgeous. Where on earth did you get this?"

"I picked it up years ago at a kitschy consignment shop in the Village. Only wore it once to a friend's wedding."

"May I try it on?"

"Of course!" I step out to give her privacy, and hop up on my bed. "Can I ask you something?" I request through the closed door. "Why a Givency dress?"

"I'll explain in a minute. First, can you zip me up?" The door slowly swings open, and she sashays over to me.

"This dress was made for you, Liv. I mean it, it never looked half as elegant on me. Fortunate for you, I have no boobs either, so it fits like a glove." I direct her to the floor-length mirror in the corner.

"It's lovely. This is really too much, are you sure?"

I insist.

"You asked why a Givency dress," she states, while admiring her reflection. "I was thirteen when I moved up here from Georgia. It was the early sixties, and the Civil Rights movement was in full swing – a tumultuous time to be a black girl, especially down south. Schools were just beginnin' to desegregate, and the quality of education in our small town had crumbled under the pressure.

"My mother raised me as a single parent, and struggled to put food on our table. Such a sharp, strong woman too, but because she wasn't formally educated, couldn't gain employment that was anythin' beyond menial. She had the vision to recognize that in the changin' social climate, opportunities would exist for me as they never had for her. However, in order for me to take full advantage of them, I had to leave home, I had to leave her. It was an agonizin' decision, sendin' me to live with my cousin Cecelia and her husband in Brooklyn, so I could go to the same private school as their kids.

"The day before I boarded the train, I snuck in the back door of the only movie theatre in town to catch a double feature of *West Side Story* and *Breakfast at Tiffany's*. Both were set in New York City, and I was anxious to see how different my new life up north was going to be. And boy, did I take Hollywood seriously. I half expected to see a street fight between the Jets and the Sharks when I stepped out of Penn Station." She giggles at the memory.

"Anyway, I fell in love with the little black dress Audrey Hepburn wears in the opening scene of *Breakfast at Tiffany's*. One day, when I graduated college and became successful, I'd be able to buy a dress like that. I dreamed about the opulent parties where I would wear it, how exquisite the fabric would feel, and the dapper gentleman who would notice me from across the room and resolve to make me his wife.

"Needless to say, things turned out very differently. Clyde and I met in a dingy laundromat on East Third Street. He asked me out that day and I said no. I turned him down every laundry day for the next month, because whenever I was there, he was there. Clyde always swore it was a coincidence, that we were just meant to be, but I knew he went there every day to wait for me. Finally, I grew tired of his pesterin' and agreed to go on our first date, which was dinner at his momma's house because the man had spent his last dime washin' his draws, but that's neither here nor there.

"One night, shortly after my initial diagnosis, I couldn't fall asleep, so I started flippin' through the television channels. When I landed on the classic movie station, there was Ms. Hepburn, in her gorgeous dress. It was the first time I'd seen it since I was a naïve young southern girl, and was reminded of what it had once represented to me. I searched the internet the next day, and learned that it was made by Givency.

"Obviously, they don't make that exact style anymore, but when I saw the price tag of a similar dress, I considered forgettin' all about it – it cost more than I had spent on my entire wardrobe in probably ten years time! Yet, see, it was fate that possessed me to add it to my list. Do you realize this is almost the exact same dress she wore in the film?" Liv spins around to face me, and puts her hands on her hips.

"Really? I've never even seen it. Hold on." I pull my MacBook from under the bed and do a Google image search of *"Breakfast at Tiffany's dress."*

"Holy crap, Liv, you're right. It's identical! You're missing a few things though." I dive back into my closet and rummage through the bins on the top shelf until I come up with a strand of faux pearls and a pair of elbow length black satin gloves. Relics from a flapper costume worn many a Halloweens ago, and my senior prom, respectively.

I accessorize her and step back to admire my work. "Now the look's complete. All that's missing is the long cigarette holder."

"Darlin', I never smoked a day in my life. Heard it causes cancer." My insides cringe at her sarcasm, but Liv looks thrilled. She has me take a picture with her phone and send it to her kids. Before I give back the BlackBerry, I tell her, "I added my phone number to your contacts, so next time you can send a picture to me, too."

After a brief tutorial on how to attach a photo to a text message, we return to the kitchen. I pour two coffees with amaretto creamer, and hand her a pencil to cross number eight off the list.

"Would you mind filling this out as well? It's a release form for the magazine."

"Not a problem at all, dah-ling" she answers in a regal tone, as her gloved hands write with exaggerated fluidity.

I curtsy in my toga and speak in an equally dignified manner. "Come. Let us sit on the so-fah and you may bestow unto my curious intellect this anthropology research you speak of. To benefit the common readers of *The Manhattan Socialite*."

We drink coffee and chat for hours until Liv notices the time on the cable box. "Would you look at that? I've kept you up with my babbling until nearly two in the morning. Let me just change, and I'll let you get off to bed. It would be a crime to ruin this magnificent outfit with tar and smashed bugs." She flits off to the bedroom, and returns a few minutes later wearing her costume and backpack.

I walk her to the door and say, "Liv, it's been such an honor to meet you. Promise you'll call and we'll do coffee again, or lunch. I want your feedback on the story, and you have to keep me posted on the progress of that list of yours."

"The pleasure and privilege were all mine, Athena. I'll treasure your dress always. We'll talk soon, darlin'."

Through my bedroom window, I watch Liv's red cape flap gracefully behind her as the Harley crawls out of site. Whether it is the adrenaline still pumping through my veins from my first motorcycle ride, or the three cups of coffee, something has me feeling wide-awake. Sitting cross-legged on my down comforter, I stir the laptop from its slumber, and browse iTunes for one of my favorite albums, *The Miseducation of Lauryn Hill*. The words leave my fingertips effortlessly as I add to *My Reflections*.

> Week 6 - Liv:
> <u>Wonder Woman</u>
> Feeling of freedom on a motorcycle
> Olive tree – symbol of peace and triumph
> Fuck it list
> "Each day is an irreplaceable opportunity"

When I am finished with this, I go back and read what I have written over the course of the last month. Assess each chance encounter as Ms. Hill professes how it could all be so simple... And just like that, it all makes sense. Five unique individuals and experiences later, a common theme has emerged. It is not complicated. It is not anything I have not heard before. I just never had the proper perspective from which to understand it.

It is simply that the value of life, that it's meaning, is exactly what you make it. And no matter the circumstances that surround it, each day should be lived completely, openly, passionately; with faith and without fear. From this modest epiphany, a hundred thoughts rush at me at once.

This experiment started by questioning what other people desire, what leads them to happiness. I was on the right track in thinking that a commitment to a goal is tied to a sense of fulfillment. Yet it is not the goal or the external validation of reaching a defined end point that is important. It is the internal process that gets you there.

Knowing exactly what you want, owning your desire, and seeing it through. Like, Theo's notebook, for example. While the finished product of his song writing was this amazing, tangible proof of his talent, the process itself is what qualified his efforts. It is his driving force for being, and what gives his life meaning. It is what makes him happy.

Applying this logic to my own life, I was looking at things all wrong when I saw my existence as the sum of my achievements. I was wrong to question why the things that were supposed to bring me happiness failed to, when what I should have been questioning was why I chose to do these things in the first place. It was the passion and process behind attaining these goals, such as my career, that held the key to my happiness, not the ends in themselves. I was so focused on the destination, my nose buried so deeply in the roadmap, in the outline, that I could not see or feel the joy the journey was meant to bring.

The truth is that this journey called life, unlike my column, or my budget, or my projects, should not be structured by a perfectly organized outline where feelings and actions are reduced to bullet points. They are meant to be felt and lived, not summarized and bounded. Likewise, I have been so caught up on judging myself based on who I think I should be, for not having the perfect feelings or the perfect relationship, that I have in turn neglected to appreciate the beautifully flawed person that I am. By over thinking the superficial, I have overlooked my true self, and failed to challenge this Athena to be better.

So... how do I live in a more fulfilled way? By taking a page out of Olivia's book. If something appeals to me, no matter how crazy or random, I need to try it. I will start my own list. Work on overcoming my fears, and turning off my daily autopilot. Stop being consumed by routine, wrapped up in getting to the end of each day while life literally passes by. Be open to and consciously seeking new experiences. Trust that my inclinations will lead to inspiration, or at least to fun, or at the very least, to a funny memory. The thing is, for the first time in my life I do not need to make shit complicated in order to feel that I have succeeded. I mean, my column was changed in only one small way, yet so much has followed – new friends, invaluable lessons, and a fresh perspective. All results from a minor inflection from the usual.

Just as the olive tree brought the end to a war among gods, Liv has enabled me to survive and conquer the war within myself. She was hoping that her story would inspire someone facing their own mortality, and so it begins with its author. I close the laptop, reach for the BlackBerry, and begin my list with the first thing that comes to mind. Still wearing the Wonder Woman crown, I turn off the light to sleep. Although this evening has left me feeling a million times lighter and stronger, you never know when your dreams will require you to be invincible.

*****

"Athena Wallace, you better have a good fucking reason for blowing off happy hour for the last few weeks. So, take your reclusive ass on an extended lunch, and tell me all about it over drinks at The Bleu Martini – I just earned at least a three hour break."

"Please, please do not elaborate on how. And, I know, Nay. I'm sorry, I've been so caught up with work, but I can't today, my phone's been ringing off the hook about the column that just dropped. I really would love it, though, if you and George, and Lori and Michael would come out with me tomorrow night. To Prose Lounge, in NoHo. Can you make it?"

Nadine sighs heavily into the phone, and replies in a ho-hum voice, "Sure, girl, I'll be there. But do I *have* to bring my husband?"

"You don't *have* to. I just thought it would be nice to all get together."

"Alright, I'll bring his raggedy ass along, but –"

The sound of Mark's voice through the intercom cuts our conversation short. "Another call regarding Taj Sharma, Athena. I transferred the last two to Brian."

"Damn, that's like the twentieth call this morning. Thanks, you can pass it through. Sorry, Nay, I have to take this. See you tomorrow." I hang up my cell and pick up the office phone. "This is Athena."

"Hi Athena, it's Vince Martucci."

"Vince! How are you? What'd you think of your story? And how's everything going with Theresa?"

"Theresa and I are awesome, and the shop's never been busier. We can't thank you enough. That's actually what I'm calling about. Since the article came out, we're having a hard time keeping up with cleaning and maintenance. When I read about the cabbie looking for a part-time job, I thought 4Brooklyn Mechanics could help him out."

"That's so nice of you, but Taj has already accepted another position."

"Damn, that's too bad. Good for him, though, seems like a decent dude."

"He is. Thank you so much for calling, it was great to hear from you. Tell Theresa and the boys I say hello."

"Will do. Later."

Before I even take my hand off the handset Mark buzzes again. "Another call for you, dear." He passes it through.

"This is Athena."

"Athena, it's Ashley from The Shack."

"Hey Ashley, what's up? I apologize if my photographer was pushy the other night, but he did get some great shots of the costume contest. You calling to get the lowdown on the review, or to tell me you landed that modeling agency gig and want to offer Taj your bartending job?"

"What? No, listen, I'm really sorry to bother you at work, but there's something I think you should know. I overheard you talking about writing a story on Liv, and saw you leave the bar with her. Not sure if you've heard, but, um, Athena, my manager just called to tell me that she passed away a couple days ago."

Oh no. No, no, no. Not her. Not now. My heart crashes into my gut. I rest my elbows on the desk to keep from keeling over. "The wake is tonight, all of us from the bar are going. I can give you the details if you want."

"Yes, please, Ashley," I push the words through my tightened throat. I stare at the address of the funeral home through a pool of tears, not fully comprehending the drying ink's poignancy, until a deep voice rumbles through the haze.

"You should be ecstatic to learn that I'm back on assignment with you. So, what mind-blowing Manhattan hotspot are you taking me to this week?" Anthony notices my expression and steps into my office, the golden rings in his eyes radiating concern. "Hey, you all right?" He asks.

I sniff and wipe away the tears. "Yeah, I'm okay. You missed out on meeting a truly amazing woman last Saturday." I slip the post-it into my purse, and compose myself. "This week is Prose Lounge. Best open mic night in the city."

"I have actually been there."

"No way."

"Yes, and I agree. You'll definitely find someone with depth to write about." I smile slightly at his intuition. "Athena, about why I was pulled off the assignment –"

"It's for you again," Mark announces through the intercom. Anthony paces for a few minutes, then examines the framed vodka bottle I had autographed by Diddy at a Peach Cîroc release party, while I explain to the long-winded caller that Taj has already gained employment and graciously thank her for the offer.

"Anyway, what I was saying –" This time it is Brian who interrupts him.

"I trust that Anthony's told you he's back with you on *The Scene*? Make sure you inform Freddie you won't be needing him tomorrow night." Brian steps into my office and looks sideways at the cactus on my desk. He turns his back to Anthony and takes a seat, insinuating that his presence is no longer welcome.

"So, uh, what time tomorrow?" Anthony asks.

"Around nine."

"See you then." Anthony disappears, his mystery and cologne lingering.

"Athena," Brian begins. "Can I just say what a fantastic job you have done with this series? I knew you were the right person to kick this thing off. You took my concept to heights that far exceeded my expectations. Over the last few issues, you've really showcased your journalism skills, which believe me, haven't gone unnoticed with the higher-ups. Your future is very bright at *The Socialite*. Anyway, I'll sing your praises more in the writer's meeting, but I wanted to tell you personally how thrilled I am with the results."

"Thank you, Brian, I appreciate you trusting me to take the lead with it. I got a lot out of this assignment, too."

"So, who's the soul of the city this week?" he asks while rising.

"Actually, I need to talk to you about that. I wrote about a very inspiring woman named Olivia. Unfortunately, I just got the news that she lost her battle with breast cancer." I pause and sigh, still not believing the words that have just crossed my lips. "Out of respect, I'll have to ask her family's permission to run the story when I'm at the wake tonight."

"I'm sorry to hear that. Send it to editing anyway, and if the family says no, we'll use only the review portion and add an ambiguous line stating why." He glances at his digital watch with indifference. "See you in the conference room in ten." When Brian is out the door, I buzz Mark.

"You can forward any other calls that come in today to my voicemail. Annnd, if you don't have plans tomorrow evening, you can meet us out at Prose in NoHo, at nine."

"Hmmm. The drag queen bar where you met the rich gay starlet you say nothing about, but a sports bar, aka hetero headquarters, you deem fit for an invitation? You offend me."

"It's not a sports bar, it's a lounge. Very urban meets avant-garde. P-R-O-S-E," I spell out for him.

"I see. Will Anthony be there?"

"Yes."

"Then I will gladly join you. By the way, did you ever find out what the deal was with him?"

"No, and I'm shocked that you didn't either. You're in a dry spell lately. I may have to revoke your designation as office Oprah."

Mark gasps. "Never that! Gail, I gotta go, Studman needs me." I hear Anthony in the background asking for the key to the supply closet as the speaker clicks off.

The column I put the final touches on this morning is up on my computer screen, and I don the Ray Bans to review it one more time before adding an addendum.

In loving memory of Olivia Williams, the real life Wonder Woman.

*****

I am the last to take a seat in the meeting, and Mario the sandwich guy flashes his customary creepy smile as he brushes past. I pretend to be too preoccupied chomping on my apple and reading the nutrition facts of a 100 calorie pack of Sun Chips to notice.

My boss clears his throat in front of the dry erase board that still has *Souls of the City* underlined three times on it.

"Happy Friday, people. Let's get started. As you all know, we are in the final stages of Athena's *Come Here Often* series. Four have been printed, and the feedback has been overwhelmingly positive. This week's issue alone has generated an unprecedented response from our readers. I couldn't be prouder of Athena for the way she handled the curve ball I threw at her. She's knocked it out of the park, don't you agree?"

My co-workers are coerced into clapping, and the forced accolade makes me uncomfortable. "After this week, *The Scene* will return to its status quo, at least for now. I'd like us to spend the bulk of our time today brainstorming whose column should be next to tackle this," he taps his knuckle on the board, "and whether we follow Athena's template exactly or take a different approach."

While the other writers toss around ideas, I stare out the bay window at the New York skyline and allow the painful reality of Liv's passing to sink in.

*****

The train shakes my body side to side as it rumbles on its tracks. I am texting Lori directions to the bar for tomorrow night, when a woman steers her stroller forcefully into my ankle. I prepare to give her the evil eye, but am intercepted by the toothless smile of the sweetest little baby boy sporting a Yankees pinstripe cap.

"He's adorable," I say to his mother, then stand to give her my seat. At this moment, on the way to say goodbye to Liv, I realize there would be no more suitable tribute to her than to get started on my list. There is only item on it so far, which I am a few days away from completing. I navigate out of text messages into the notepad app, and type number two.

Go to a Yankees game.

I have had plenty of opportunities to score free tickets since I started at *The Socialite*, but could never find a date worthy of the experience (my ex was neither a fan of sports or spending quality time with me). So, I will have to take myself, or casually remind Nadine how formfitting their uniforms are. The smell of the subway station gyro wafting from the next row of seats over gives me another idea.

Number three: *Learn how to make spanakopita.*

My mother is always offering to teach me, I suspect in an attempt to get me to cook thus building my marriage marketability, but I presumed myself too impatient for filo dough. Which gives rise to number four.

Go to Greece.
No.
Take my mom to Greece.

This inspires number five.
Learn about my African roots.

I scan my surroundings for further inspiration. Sitting across from me is an older gentleman, wearing an old-school Kangol newsboy cap and the black counterpart to my glasses. He is buried in a literary classic I remember falling in love with in high school.

Number six: *Read To Kill a Mockingbird again.*

Above his head is an ad for one of the food shows that I record and usually watch, admittedly hypocritically, while my nightly take-out is either being delivered or re-heated – it stimulates my appetite, like food foreplay. That fact paired with my senseless celebrity crush on Clinton Kelly leads to number seven.

Be an audience member on The Chew.

Ooo... and *sit at the tasting table on Meatless Monday.*
The adjoining ad is for a seasonal collection of coffee creamers. This one is going to be hard, but I will give it a shot.

Number eight: *Try pumpkin spice creamer in my coffee.*

The speakers ding as the conductor indistinguishably announces the next stop.

Number nine: *Ice skate in Rockefeller Center at Christmastime.*

Another iconic New York experience I have denied myself as an adult by either dating duds or being too wrapped up in my singleness. By the time I reach my destination, there are fourteen items on my list. Well, fifteen, but I manage to delete *"Get over irrational fear of birds"* only a few minutes after adding it by forcing myself to touch a slow moving, obese pigeon. Poor girl probably just went through a bad break up with a smooth talking woodpecker who played her then flew south for the winter.

"He's not worth the calories, sister," I empathize, before racing into a nearby convenience store and dousing myself with an entire mini bottle of Purell. I am proud of my progress, but at this rate, I will have to include "quit my job" to make any headway.

Outside of the funeral home, motorcycles intermix with Prius's embellished with Darwin fish bumper stickers and chromed out Cadillacs with Georgia license plates. Inside, the people are as eclectic as the parking lot suggests. I spot

Ashley, whose hair color has changed to powder pink, and give her a slight wave as I take my place at the end of the long, winding line. Well over an hour passes before I enter the room. Standing off to the side is a young girl, maybe seven or eight, wearing three braids secured with those elastic hair ties with balls on the end that I used to wear when I was her age. She is singing gospel hymns a cappella, her voice as moving and powerful as it is raw and innocent.

"Amazing grace, how sweet the sound
That saved a wretch like me"

At the front of the line a tall, impeccably dressed man who appears to be around my age offers a firm handshake. "Thank you for coming. I'm Solomon, Olivia's son. And you are?"

"I'm Athena. I only recently met your mother, but her amazing spirit left a huge impression on me. I am so, so sorry for your loss." His face and grip both soften a bit.

"Are you the Athena who interviewed my mom for that magazine?"

"I am. She told you about that?"

"She couldn't say enough about you. You know, you left quite the impression on her as well. Aisha, this is Athena, the journalist mom was talking about." The equally striking and statuesque woman standing next to him, clutching a wad of damp tissues, leans over to embrace me.

"I am so glad you are here. Thank you for what you did for her," she says. My bottom lip begins to tremble, but I pull it together by the time Aisha releases me.

"I was hoping to meet you today. I found this on mom's desk." Solomon reaches into the interior pocket of his three-piece suit jacket and hands me a sealed envelope inscribed with my name and address. "If we didn't cross paths, I was going to send it in the mail."

"What is it?" I ask.

"Probably a thank you letter. As academic and forward thinking as our mother was, she was always the proper southern lady at heart."

"Thank you for this. Are you sure it's okay to publish her story? It hasn't gone to print yet, so it's no problem to –"

"She would have insisted," Aisha says. I smile and hold the envelope to my chest.

"She has a beautiful voice," I say, referring to the child who bares a strong resemblance to her.

Aisha nods solemnly. "She's going to miss her grandmother very much… It was lovely to meet you, Athena."

Kneeling before the open casket, I close my eyes and attempt a prayer, but the words escape me. So instead, I meditate on my sole memory of her, on the positive emotions evoked by the few hours we spent together. I make the sign of the cross and take a deep breath before glancing down. There lies Olivia, looking at peace and oh so elegant in her Givency dress.

*****

It is only after unwinding with a container of chana masala and some mindless reality TV, that I am able to bring myself to open the envelope. I lie on my closet floor and delicately peel back the gold filigree lining. Inside is a notecard embossed with the letter 'O', containing the most impeccable cursive I have ever seen.

Dear Goddess,

Thank you for the pleasure of your company the other evening, and especially for the incomparable dress. I hope I have provided enough material for your story; if not, please take the liberty of embellishing upon my good qualities.

Looking forward to being girlfriends.
Love, Olive Tree

P.S. I realize I may have misspoke in regard to my metaphor. It is you, my dear, who is a gift.

No, you were a gift, Olivia, more than you will ever know.

ized, making an organized effort, and maintaining a positive outlook on life!

CHAPTER 8

A gift?"
"Yes, from me and Tila. It is just a small thing we saw while shopping for spices at the Indian market."

Wrapped with newspaper written in a foreign script is a bracelet made of a rubber cord, strung through a one-inch colorful glass tile pendant. On the pendant is a fierce looking woman with skin the color of indigo, her enormous tongue jetting out of her mouth. She is wearing a necklace made of skulls, and holding a sword and a severed head in two of her four hands.

"That is the Hindu goddess Kali. She is called 'the dark one,' but do not mistake her for evil. Kali is the goddess of time and change," Taj explains.

"What is she doing?" I ask.

"There are many interpretations of this image, and many symbols within it. For one, her sword represents knowledge, while the man's head she is holding symbolizes the Ego, which she has killed to attain Moksha. In English, I am not so sure of this meaning..." Taj honks at another cab that is sneaking into our lane while contemplating an explanation. "Moksha is freedom from the cycle of rebirth and death. It is true consciousness, the highest happiness. Do you understand?"

Before I can answer, he inserts a disclaimer. "Please do not feel that I am trying to make you a Hindu, miss. I know from your dress on the holiday that you have an interest in goddesses, so I was believing you would enjoy this."

"I do, very much. Thank you, Taj, you didn't have to get me anything." I clasp the bracelet around my wrist and reach into my tote bag. "And I hope *you* enjoy these." I toss five copies of the latest issue of *The Socialite* onto the front seat.

"The story was very nice. You know, I am famous now. Many of my passengers wish to talk to me about my life, and I have made nearly one week of tips in just two days time! Also, have you heard that I am to start the new job at your magazine on Monday?"

"That's great, Taj! We must have gotten fifty phone calls already about job leads for you, too." He looks at me in the rear-view mirror, wide-eyed. "So, if the truck driver thing doesn't work out, I have the name of a lady who's looking to train a masseuse at her doggie day spa."

"Masseuse?"

"Someone who rubs the dogs' muscles, so they can relax and de-stress."

"Only in America," he replies with a chuckle.

The cab slows in front of the familiar row of brownstones. "This is my parents', the one with the red door. You'll pick me up in exactly two hours, right?" I reiterate.

"Yes, miss. At eight-thirty precisely."

As I walk through the living room that has not seen so much as a new throw pillow in three decades, my nose is treated to the comforting smells of my childhood. The unfiltered sounds of Smokey Robinson on vinyl ricochet off my eardrums from a *Miracles* album spinning on the antique turntable ... *Ooo, that feels so good.* There is no doubt my love of music was inherited from and nurtured by my father. *I have to get back into some Motown*, I think, as I brush my hand along a row of records in one of the three huge bookshelves I pass on the way to the kitchen.

I find my mother in her usual spot at the butcher-block island, her dark brown waves pulled into a loose bun. She is stuffing roasted peppers with cooked bulgur and fresh herbs snipped from the array of mason chairs on the windowsill above the sink. There is not one fleck of gray on her fifty-three-year-old head yet, which she swears she does not dye, and her Mediterranean skin is as radiant and taut as I always remember it being.

"Sam!" she yells out the window, while wiping her hands on her "Greeks Do It Better" apron. "Our daughter's alive! You can tell your friends at the precinct to take her face off the milk cartons!"

"Hi to you too, Mom," I say, kissing her on each cheek. "And it hasn't been that long. We talked on the phone a few days ago."

"Not that long? You haven't come home in over three months! For all I know you could've been calling from the trunk of an abductor's car."

"Yeah, because I would have forgotten to mention that."

She swats her hand at me. "At least if a man was occupying your time you'd have an excuse..." *And so it begins.*

"Leave her alone, Angela, if you want her coming around more," my father chastises her from the doorway that leads out to the patio. It pains me that, unlike my mother, he looks a little older every time I see him. I suppose it's the consequence of working such a stressful job for so long.

"Thank you," I say, before noticing his attire of oven mitts and an apron that has a picture of The David on it – all the pale naked body parts lining up with his own. "Ew Daddy, can you please not wear that in front of me?"

"What? It was a retirement present from your mom, along with the new fancy grill out there, and a very thoughtful one at that." I shield my eyes as he rubs up on my mother from the back and kisses her neck.

"Well it's gross, and it makes you look like you have some weird Michael Jackson disease." He outstretches his arms and shimmy's over to give me a hug. Holding my torso away from his, I giggle and say, "You're crazy! So, how is it being at home all day? Mom got you ironing your socks and vacuuming the ceilings?"

Her head yells at me from inside the oven. "Athena, you better stop making fun, because you know you're destined to turn into me one day."

"I'm just kidding. Come here a sec, I want to show you something." I plop my bag onto the kitchen counter and fish out the glossy plastic folder from the travel agency where I spent the better part of the morning.

"What's this?" she asks when I hand it to her, pulling her reading glasses down from the top of her head.

"You and I are taking a ten-day trip to Greece. We'll fly into Thessaloniki, that's near where your family lives, right? The plane tickets are open ended, but I was thinking we could go sometime in the spring, just let me know when and I'll schedule the time off. We'll stay the first three nights at this amazing hotel and spa the travel agent recommended. And for the rest of the time, I thought it would be fun to rent a car, and map out the places we want to explore together."

She covers her mouth and reacts in a way that is extremely out of character – she is speechless.

"That's wonderful, babygirl! I've always wanted to take her there, but you beat me to it."

"Sorry Daddy, it's a girl's only trip. Are you going to be okay having the house all to yourself for that long?"

He puts his hands on his hips and sticks his neck out. "Oh mah goodnehhhssss, it's gonna be all dat and a bag of chips!"

"Huh?" I am taken aback by my father sounding all Sheneneh Jenkins, and this gets my mother talking again.

"You asked what he's been doing in his retirement. Watching reruns everyday on TV One. His new thing is quoting that show with Martin Lawrence, and the one with the Queen, what's her name, Latifah? I tell him he sounds like an idiot but he doesn't listen."

"Hey, I've waited thirty-five years to have my afternoon stories. Stop sweatin' me, woman, and let me enjoy them! You know why?" He sings every word of the *Living Single* theme song, off tune, and does the same embarrassing pop and lock routine he first busted out when he volunteered to do security at my eighth grade formal – "... Wit my homegirls standin' to my left and my right..." – he points to my mother and me – "... Check check check it out, check check check it out." I bury my head in my hands as he pop and locks his head through the open door to sniff the air before popping it back inside. "Lamb's almost ready. How do you want yours cooked, Athena?"

"First of all, please don't ever do that again. Second of all, I've been a vegetarian since I was ten, Daddy. Why do you always insist on asking me that?"

"Because one of these days the smell of my sumptuous grilling's going to finally break you down and you'll forget all about your passion for Brussels sprouts. Put some meat on those beautiful bones." He shakes a mitt at me before disappearing to tend to the meat.

"You and your animal rights activism," my mother says, rolling her eyes.

"I'm not an activist, Mom, it's just a personal preference," I explain for the umpteenth time. "Sooo... what do you think? You're going to Greece!" I shriek and shake her shoulders, freeing a few tendrils of her hair, in an attempt to rally her enthusiasm.

"I think I have the best daughter anyone could ask for. This is too much, Athena."

"No it's not. You just have to promise to contact your relatives to plan a visit, and that you'll show me around where you used to live." She shakes her head in disbelief and smiles, flipping through the brochure that was in the folder.

"The last time I was in Polichni I was a little girl! Everything's going to look so different, I bet. So big! But I am very excited. *Oh my God*, I hope my Greek's up to par. I can't wait to call my cousin Idola and tell her we're coming. I clip your column and send it to her all the time, you know. She was my best friend when we were kids, I haven't seen her in decades! Your Aunt Katherine's going to be so jealous!" She exclaims with more pride than empathy, no sooner than barking, "But what's the occasion, why did you do this? It must have cost a fortune!"

"It really wasn't that bad, and I did it because I wanted to. You deserve it, we both do! Shoot, I haven't left the country since spring break my senior year of college," I recall, as I nibble on a kalamata olive that has been soaking in a small dish of oil.

"Don't remind me. I remember the heartburn like it was yesterday from worrying about you dancing topless in some wild orgy bar."

"I built houses for needy families in Belize, Mom."

"What? They don't have bars in Belize?" she says, while retrieving my dinner from the oven.

She sets the glass casserole dish on a blue and white hot plate in front of me, and hands over the matching Greek flag potholders. "I really can't believe it. I'm going to have to sell a lot of houses between now and springtime to afford all the jewelry and souvenirs I plan on buying. Do you think the airline allows two suitcases?"

"I'm sure it's not a problem, even if we have to pay a little extra. How's the market anyway, are sales picking up?"

"Way up. I'm back to almost full-time hours again." She checks behind her before pinching her thumb and pointer finger together and whispering, "And maybe your father's driving me a little bit nutzo being home all the time, too."

"I'm almost glad you won't eat this, babygirl, because that means there's more deliciousness for me!" my father says as he bursts through the door with a steaming rack of lamb.

"Go put the peppers on the table, and here's some forks and napkins," my mother instructs, shooing me into the dining room. It is nothing short of a tragedy in this house for a meal to dip below scalding hot before being consumed.

The gold-rimmed plates are already stacked in the middle of the table along with three glasses of water with melted ice cubes. I set a place for each of us on the lace tablecloth. As I do so, I study the grade school pictures of me hanging against the flowered wallpaper, each year with progressively higher and frizzier bangs. Thank goodness I eventually discovered a flat iron, thus allowing me to have some type of sex life, even if it is currently non-existent.

"Mom," I moan when she comes in with two large platters of food, "why do you still have these photos here? Can't they go in the attic somewhere?"

"Well, I've been waiting to replace them with some wedding pictures, which seemed imminent until you ended it with that nice, handsome boy, Damon..."

The ease at which my ex's name rolls off my mother's tongue irks me. I never told her the real reason that relationship ended, because part of me knew she would question what I did to lead him into the arms of another woman. Her grief was the last thing I needed while trying to deal with my own.

"Angela!" my dad warns from behind the kitchen door.

"How can he even hear me?" she asks.

"Maybe it's because you were born without an inside voice? Remind me to pack earplugs for our trip. If it's a cultural thing,

I don't want to come back deaf," I say, relieved to be on to a new topic.

My dad grunts in acquiescence and takes his place at the head of the table.

"Anyway," she backpedals while serving us each a healthy portion of tomato feta salad, "that reminds me. Did you ever call Dr. Dulong?"

"Daddy, you feeling okay?" I ask before he can answer her.

My mother forces her chin against her neck and glares at me as I size up my father with worry.

"I knew you were just appeasing me by taking his phone number," she says.

"Oh, you were talking to me?" I ask, then recall her latest attempt to fix me up. "That's right, the veterinarian! I lost the paper where I wrote it down."

"That's okay! I found someone even better. He's a new client, who runs a very successful personal training business, only divorced once I think, half Italian, which is almost as good as being part Greek, and searching for – get this – a three bedroom condo in a family friendly building because he plans on *having children someday*!" She is close to shouting the last three words.

"Athena doesn't want no muscle head Italian man. What she needs is a funny, handsome, down-to-earth brother like her father. Which I'm sure she is perfectly capable of finding on her own." My father grins at me and sucks dry the bone he is holding.

"I appreciate the input into my love life, thank you both very much, but I really am just fine being single right now." My father hums the sitcom theme song again while taking hot sauce out of his sweat pants pocket, and the sight of him shaking it onto his rack of lamb distracts my mother from nagging me for the time being.

"Sam, stop it! That does *not* belong on my perfectly seasoned lamb. You and that damn Tabasco." He blows her a kiss to egg her on. Seriously, this same scenario has played out over every meal ever eaten at this table. Remembering what else happened the last time I ate here, my chewing comes to a halt.

"You didn't sneak meat in here again, right? I still haven't forgiven you for that," I say to my mother.

"No, eat, eat! You just looked so skinny and sickly, I figured a little chicken skin couldn't hurt," she replies, slapping two more peppers onto my plate. "I'm afraid you're going to get cancer from all the microwaved food you eat." She could not know how insensitive the timing of her statement is, probably misquoting her precious Dr. Oz – who, and I quote, "is brilliant and Turkish thus practically Greek" – so I use my thoughts of Liv to change the subject.

"Daddy, I've been meaning to ask you about that 'Black to Africa' study you did at NYU. Did you ever follow up with it?"

"What's there to follow up on? They took a DNA sample, mailed me a paper with the results, and that was it. Only reason I did it was because your Uncle Derrick was dating that 'anti-establishment,'" he uses air quotes, "college girl with all the hair."

"I didn't know that.... What do you mean by 'all the hair?'" I ask.

"It was everywhere, on her legs, her armpits, above her upper lip... She coaxed him into participating in the study, and he begged me to go with him to hold his pansy-ass hand because he thought he had to get blood drawn. One step inside the health center and he passed out, so I did the test for him. Turns out all they had to do was swab the inside of my cheek."

I gag when he says swab, a reflex resulting from the date with the STD-free mascot I met online months ago.

"Derrick ended up catching that chick waxed and enjoying a latte at Starbucks with some NBA player a few days later, so needless to say, the test results were of no interest to him. Don't you remember, he went through that pan-Africanism phase last summer? Wait, I think I still have a picture of him at the family reunion."

My father's philandering, Kevin-Hart-sized youngest brother is always the butt of his four older brothers' jokes, due to the fact that he has a tendency to overcompensate for his lack of height and common sense by going out of his way to please his woman du jour. One time, back in the eighties, he was trying to holler at the vice-president of the Lionel Ritchie fan club, and my mother gave us boxed Jheri curls together in the downstairs bathroom. I ended up resembling a poodle and he lost half his hair, which never did end up growing back.

"I'm wrapping your leftover peppers up for you to take home," my mother insists after my father goes into the living room to search for the photo.

"No, please don't. I'm going out from here and I don't want anything to leak into my purse," I plead.

"The Tupperware is airtight, you're taking it." Sizing up my leggings, college sweatshirt with ripped collar, and sneakers, she adds, "You're not going out looking like that are you?"

"Really, Mom? You know me better than that. I have a change of clothes in that big bag, which I'll pick up next time I'm over. As much as I love your food, I don't need to go to the bar smelling like it."

"You sure? Maybe you'd attract a man who'd think you cook."

Now how does she twist every little thing I say like that? *I am lucky to have her love and concern in my life,* I remind myself as I bite down on my tongue.

After helping her clear the table, I head upstairs. When I open the door to the room where I plan on getting ready, I am surprised to discover that, unlike the rest of the house, my old bedroom has been completely revamped. A sixty-inch flat screen hangs in place of my Tevin Campbell posters, which are rolled up on top of the dresser, and an oversized power recliner is where my canopy bed used to be.

There is also a mini-fridge stocked with tapioca cups and Heinekens. Figuring I might as well make the best of a surprising situation, I use a badge shaped talking bottle opener that says, "police, open up" to crack the cap off one to sip while getting ready.

"Gurrrl, that outfit is *da bomb*," my father says as I skip down the stairs, pausing midway to shake my head disapprovingly at him. He has replaced the Miracles with Earth, Wind & Fire, and has a photo album open in his lap.

"Hope you don't mind, I stole one of the beers out of your man-cave, a.k.a. my former room. I brought you one, too." I hand it to him and place my empty one on an end table, then take a seat on the arm of his well-worn chair. "Nice TV, by they way. I'm surprised Mom let you do all that."

"This is my house too, she doesn't control me," he says under his breath. I give him the *stop playin'* look, and he adds, "Ask to see her new diamond earrings."

"Mmm hmm, that sounds more accurate. Did you find it?" He points to a picture of my Uncle Derrick with a Marcus Garvey t-shirt and what can only be described as a half-fro.

"Looks like a Chia Pet got attacked by a gopher," he comments, resulting in a shared belly laugh over the poor man's bald spots.

"Oh, I'm going to ruin my makeup," I say, wiping away the tears. "I see you've had time to finally organize all those boxes of pictures. What else is in here?" We flip through photographs from semi-annual Wallace reunions in the Park, which occur with such frequency that you do not have a chance to miss any damn body, laughing at my uncle's outrageous fashion choices over the years.

"Anyone want coffee with dessert?" my mother calls out from the kitchen.

"No thanks, I have to get going. My cab will be here any minute," I holler back.

My father stands and a paper that must have been tucked into the back of the album falls to the floor. He unfolds it, and gives it to me.

"Here, it's the results of that study. You seem interested in learning about your heritage all of a sudden. By, the way, that's really something, what you did for your mom."

"It's for both of us," I clarify.

"No dessert? But I went *all* the way to the bakery in Bay Ridge to pick up some baklava for you, it's your fav-or-ite!" My mother's words ooze with guilt, just as a loud honk comes from the street.

"That's my ride, I really have to go."

"Then take a few pieces with you." She dashes back to the kitchen, and my father gives me a big kiss.

"It's good to see you, babygirl. You should come around for dinner more often. Your mom would like that."

"Good to see you too, Daddy. I will. Mom and I have a vacation to plan!" I say, as she returns with a Ziploc bag full of sticky pastries and the container of leftovers I was forgetting on purpose. "Now where do you expect me to put all that?"

"Here." She shoves the goods into my purse, and they stick out of the top.

"At least hold on to the baklava, it'll keep until next weekend, right? I'll come over on Sunday and we can start Googling things to do in Greece." This appeases her and she takes the bag back.

"I'll make spanakopita, maybe you can finally watch and learn. And thank you again for the trip, it's way too much." She pecks both my cheeks.

"See you next Sunday. Love you Mom, love you Daddy."

*****

Taj is enjoying the last bite of his vegetarian Greek dinner as he pulls up to Prose Lounge. Mark is just arriving too, and we walk in together.

"Friend or faux?" Mark asks while helping me out of my fox fur jacket.

I frown. "It's not faux."

"Oh honey, this is a judgment free zone." He swirls his fingers around his face. "I just bought a new chinchilla muff that has me absolutely aching for winter. It's the perfect accouterment to my eel skin boots."

"What?"

"It means an accessory, an ac-cou-tre-ment," he pronounces slowly.

"Boy, I'm not remedial. I was just curious as to why the hell you need a muff. Never mind." We both giggle immaturely at the reference. "Anyway, it's vintage couture, made before I was born. If anything, I've elongated its time on earth." Mark hangs the coat on the back of a metal barstool, as I re-tuck my leopard print blouse into my red skinny jeans; a louder outfit than I usually go for, but tonight is all about pushing myself outside of my comfort zone.

We are the first ones here, so decide to share a bottle of Prosecco over some tasteless workplace gossip.

"Larry and Brian? Nuh-uh. Brian had that thing with the intern a few months ago, and Larry's been married for like twenty years, to a *woman*. I don't believe you."

"I wouldn't believe me either if I hadn't seen them with my own eyes. In the very spot he did the intern, nonetheless. I mean the desk, not the hole. It's called bisexuality my friend. The fad totally escapes me, but it's apparently what they're into. So, have I redeemed myself?" Mark asks, beaming.

"I suppose, but how is it that you always just happen to be at the exact discreet location to witness all this after hours booty calling?

I've never even seen you in the building a minute past four o'clock." He shrugs his shoulders and raises his eyebrows demurely, and I suck my teeth at him. "Help me think of what to write in my review," I say, taking out the BlackBerry.

"Well, I'm *obsessed* with the whole exposed brick and pipe thing. Love the tea lights everywhere, adds a touch of warmth to the otherwise industrial space. And the artwork spray-painted on the walls – quotes from what appears to be Shakespearean literature – very cerebral thug."

"Damn, you're pretty good at this."

"I'm not just a pretty face," Mark retorts, while licking his finger to remove the excess eyebrow pencil he spots in his reflection in the ice bucket.

The sultry voice of Jill Scott singing a live version of her definitive track, "A Long Walk", plays oh so fluidly as my friends start to filter in.

"Where are the guys?" I ask Nadine and Lori when they sit with us at the bar.

"Parking the car," Nadine answers. Anthony is right behind them, and Mark pushes past the girls to greet him.

"Heyyyy Anthony! So good to see you. Let's leave these chicken heads to squawk while the cocks do some shots."

"I think the word you're looking for is hens?" Lori reprimands Mark, as he drags Anthony over to where the bartender is standing.

"No, I had it right," he shouts without looking back. "Yoo hoo, can I get two slippery nipples?" The three of us shake our heads.

"You know what he's trying to do, right?" I ask.

"I know exactly what he's trying to do," Lori says, and Nadine sighs melodramatically.

"I'm sorry Athena, and I swear I won't bring it up again, but it's a damn shame all that fineness is wasted on a vagina that doesn't belong to one of us." My back is to him, but I turn my head just enough to catch Anthony downing a shot with Mark out of the corner of my eye. *Well ain't that some shit.* I brush off her comment, signaling for the bartender.

"Can we have two more glasses please?"

"Just one. I'll take an ice water," Lori interjects.

"When are you due?" Nadine asks flatly, and my head whips from her to Lori.

"Welll, I haven't been to the doctor or anything yet, but by our calculations sometime around the forth of July."

"But I thought...?" My eyes are about to pop out my head.

"That I was on the pill? I was until the pack went missing, right after that day you girls came for brunch," Lori explains. "I had to wait for my next cycle before filling my prescription, then when I was late, figured I should take a pregnancy test... I got so emotional waiting for the results that I finally told Michael how much I wanted to go back to school... and, after it came back positive, he broke down and confessed that he hid my pills. I didn't even know he knew I was taking them."

"So what are you going to do?" I ask intensely, pouring Nadine and myself the sparkling wine.

"Well, Michael felt so bad for what he did, he's picked up an extra shift at his job so I can cut way back on my hours at work and enroll in the program. I'll go to school full-time until the baby's born, then part-time until I finish. That's the plan anyway."

"Congratulations, that's wonderful. I'll tell you right now, though, I'm not babysitting it."

"What the hell, Nadine?" I say.

"I told you girls, that's what grandmothers are for. I'm done with kids. In fact, I'll sign over both of mine to either one of you right here, right now. They're almost grown, so you bypass all the potty training and shit, and you're still in time to claim the tax credit for this year. Come on, Athena, you don't want to lose your figure by being pregnant."

"So encouraging, thank you," Lori replies, crossing her arms.

"Now you know I'm just playing, girl. Children are miracles and shit, and I'm very happy for you. I'm *not* playing about the babysitting part though."

"What did George Jr. do to get your weave all in a bunch this time?" I ask.

"Let me tell you what this bad ass mother fucker did –"

"The child has a mouth like his mama, that's the real problem," George answers, as he and Michael join us.

"Congratulations, Daaaddy," Nadine says to Michael.

"You told them? I thought we were going to wait until we went to the doctor!" he whines.

"I know honey, but these are my *girls*," Lori justifies.

"Your husband told me on the walk here. Congratulations to you both, God bless." George hugs Lori, then turns his attention to me. "And Athena, thank you for inviting us all out tonight. I know it wasn't my wife's idea to bring me along." Nadine squints and smirks at him.

"You're welcome, I'm glad you guys could make it. I thought it would be nice to have all my friends out with me – to have a few drinks on *The Socialite*, and let you know how much you are loved and appreciated." I motion for the bartender to get two more glasses for the guys.

"Well, that's awful nice of you, but let's keep it real. We've all read your new series and couldn't help but speculate that you might have an ulterior motive in bringing us here tonight?" Michael says, then is jabbed by his wife's elbow. I give him a confused look.

"Bitch, are you going to write about one of us? Because if you are, I'm just putting it out there that I am the most fascinating among this group." The other three snap their necks in Nadine's direction. "I mean, how often do you come across a woman who holds it down at the office and at home, and looks this *fly* doing it? Not every day. I'm the brains, the brawns, and the booty. I'm a god damn triple threat."

"Well I'm sorry to disappoint, especially you, Miss In-Your-Own-Universe, but I'm not writing about any of you," I say.

"That's too bad, but speaking of your column... about those nudists you met. Did you happen to get a business card, or website address, or anything? My wife and I are interested in joining their club. Right, Nadine?" George asks, stroking his giant stomach.

"Ha ha! That's right baby! You know how we gets *down*."

"Puh-lease get back *up*, because no one wants to hear that shit," I articulate to them, while Lori and Michael scrunch their faces in disgust.

Michael changes the subject by engaging George in a conversation about football, and Nadine saunters over to the other two members of our entourage. Lori scoots her stool closer to mine. "I'm happy to finally catch up, even though you are technically working." She plays with my bracelet as she speaks. "Kali, the goddess of Shakti, Empowerment. We do a meditation on her in my mantra yoga class. Is this new?"

"Yes, Taj gave it to me tonight."

"It's beautiful. It suits you and this journey you've been on."

"Thank you. So, a baby?"

"A baby," she answers, reciprocating my disbelief. "I know I said I wasn't ready to start a family yet, but I'm actually *really* happy. I think I was so worried that my life was going to be put on hold that I didn't try to hear Michael out. But now that he's making it possible for me to go back to school, it feels like it was supposed to happen this way. Like everything's falling into place... It'll be a financial strain on us for a few years at least, and I'm definitely nervous about being a student again, but I feel ready for it. The energy this new life is creating within me is ethereal. I'm sure I'll change my tune when the morning sickness kicks in though."

"I'm happy for you, too, sweetie. You do look all glowy."

"You look different too, Athena. Spiritually serene. This assignment has been really good for you, huh?"

"It has." Before she can ask me to elaborate, the deejay scratches the record that is playing, and Nadine rejoins us with Mark and Anthony in tow. The emcee, whose apparel is a fusion of 70's hip-hop and punk rock, takes the stage.

"Welcome to Prose Lounge, where every night is open mic night. Looks like we have a full house here tonight, but there is still room on the roster if you are interested in performing. No experience is necessary. We are artists here to build up other artists, so don't be shy. Please see one of our bar staff and they'll be happy to add you to the lineup. Now, please join me in welcoming to the stage our first performer, and the three time reigning champion of the Borough Rap Battle. This dude is insane. Mr. Sean-y Kash everyone." "The Roots' You Got Me" plays and a scrawny white guy emerges from the audience.

"We're going to grab that last table," Michael conveys over the applause while he and George walk away from the bar.

"I'll be right there, I want to get us another bottle," I tell my friends, and all but Anthony head into the seating area. A combination of spoken-word poetry and beatboxing that caliber rivals Biz Markie's fills the room, as all head's turn to the unlikely source.

"Another bottle of Prosecco, please, and I'd like to add my name to the list." The bartender hands me the sign-up sheet and Anthony gawks at me.

"*You're* going up there?"

"Don't sound so surprised. Yes, *I'm* going up there, to read an excerpt from next week's column. The last face in the *Come Here Often* series is going to be my own."

"Okay... care to explain?"

"Well, my readers don't know anything about me, so I figured after two years I'd finally introduce myself. In addition, public speaking is one of my biggest fears, so I'm taking it on as a personal challenge as well."

"Very admirable, but you mean to tell me that hundreds of thousands of people read your words every week, yet you're afraid to recite them in front of a bar full?"

"That's correct. Terrified, actually." Anthony seems amused by my candidness, but by the way he is incessantly shifting his gaze onto everything except me, I cannot help but think that he looks nervous, too. Or maybe I am just projecting.

"I meant to mention that tonight was going to be more laid back, you could have brought Ru-nay. Sorry."

"Don't be. Athena, there's something I need to tell you," he replies.

"Is it about why you were pulled off assignment with me last week? You started saying something about it in my office the other day. What happened, anyway?"

"Well, it's kind of a long story -- "

"I'm number ten, we've got time. *Thank God*," I utter, and pour myself more liquid courage.

He holds his empty rocks glass out for me to fill, and downs nearly half of it before saying, "You remember that morning Brian called me into his office, all upset? It's because he had gotten a phone call from the cops, about what happened to Charlene."

"Charlene?"

"Yeah. They found rohypnol in her system, roofies." I lean closer to him and take a sip, enthralled by why he knows this and I do not. "She remembered that I had brought her drinks, and turned over the business card you left at the hospital to the police. That's how they knew to contact The Socialite to find me.

"Anyway, her father's some bigwig judge, and as soon as Brian released my address, a warrant was issued to search my apartment. I ran home to intercept the cops, to try to explain that I had absolutely nothing to do with what happened to her, but they beat me there. Renée let them in, and they confiscated an unmarked prescription bottle with a pill in it they found in a dresser drawer. Since it wasn't mine, I confronted Renée about it, and she swore up and down she never saw it before either. Even threatened to break up with me over it."

"Oh my God."

"It gets worse. A few days later, it was determined to be the same drug that was in Charlene's system, and charges were filed against me. We met with an attorney, who explained that *when* I was found guilty of messing with a judge's daughter, I was looking at three years jail time. That's when Renée finally broke down and confessed that the pill was hers, that she got it from her drug dealer ex-boyfriend whom she'd also been sleeping with." Anthony's nostrils flare and he takes another swig.

"But why'd she want to roofie *Charlene*?"

"She thought… she was you," he remarks regrettably, as though he is somehow accountable for her actions.

"Are you fucking kidding me?" I cannot stop myself from sounding uncouth. "Why would she want to do that?"

He leans back in his barstool and exhales forcibly.

"Renée, among other things, is the jealous type. Because *she* was creepin', she always suspected me of doing the same. After that first night I met you, I told her about what happened. You know, how you hit me in the nuts?"

My eyelids clamp down to shield me from my embarrassment, and I force the corners of my mouth up to relay that yes, I am aware of what he is referring to.

"I made it into a joke," Anthony continues, "but I guess from that point on, Renée had it out for you. Every time I talked about you, which in retrospect might have been often, it would turn into a fight. You didn't notice my phone blowing up every time we were out?" I shake my head naïvely. *He talked about me often?*

"Well, apparently she thought drugging you would cause you to act sloppy in front of me, and I'd be turned off... Or maybe her demented ass thought you would hit on me in front of her, then she could call you out on it and start some drama. Whatever the reason, you hightailed away in the club that night before I could introduce you. She brought over those shots, and only after Charlene drank it did she realize she wasn't you. She bounced before anyone was the wiser."

"Wow, that's crazy! Poor Charlene. Is she facing charges?"

"Her court appearance was Wednesday. The judge thinks she's taking the fall for me, but since they can't prove there was any intent for sexual assault, she was slapped on the wrist with ninety days community service. You know, Brian's really protective of you. He wouldn't put us back on assignment together until I was able to produce proof of the verdict," he says, his face made markedly less tense by his divulgence, his eyes finally focused on me.

"Sooo... Can I assume you two are no longer seeing each other?" *Don't seem too eager, Athena, easy bree – oh, fuck that.*

"That's putting it mildly. Her shit was on the curb the minute we got back from the lawyer's office. I guess because I was travelling so much throughout the course of our relationship, I never got to know the real her... That's it! My mother's never setting me up again."

He takes the Prosecco bottle and refills his glass.

"What's up with the drinking all of a sudden? I thought you didn't want to over *indulge* while working?" I ask.

Anthony stares into the bubbling beverage for a few seconds before exploring my eyes and replying, "Athena, alcohol has a tendency to strip away my inhibitions. I say whatever's on my mind, and act on whatever I'm feeling."

"Okay...?"

"So, when I said that, what I meant was that I was afraid of over indulging in *you*."

I have to casually put my hand on my chest to keep my heart from leaping out. *Did I just hear him right?* The next statement to leave his immaculately arched lips confirms that I did.

"I like you, Athena. Renée might be wrong in every other way possible, but she was right in her hunch about my feelings for you."

"Maybe I like you, too," is the understatement that slowly escapes me.

"What do you want to do about it?" he asks coolly, provocatively.

I tilt my gaze and consider him, my stiletto falling to the tip of my toe. "Well, we aren't working together anymore, at least for now, but I could use your professional expertise in next Saturday's review of Constellations Winebar. It's nearing the end of the rooftop season, so I probably *should* commemorate it with a romantic venue that overlooks the entire city and offers an incredible wine tasting menu for two."

"That sounds extremely appropriate, at least in my professional opinion. Just do me one favor?" he requests through a crooked smile.

Absolutely anything. "What's that?"

"Don't let your buddy Mark know that I'm, ahem, taking you out on a date. I think he's hoping to convert me to his team, and I don't want to lose my unrestricted access to the office supply closet," he jokes. "The man even special orders felt tip pens for me because he knows I don't like the cheap ballpoint ones."

"A highly coveted connection that I assure you I will not ruin." After making a cross over my heart, which is beating thunderously but remains inside my chest, it seems safe enough to move my hand. Anthony is momentarily distracted by what is taking place on stage, while I attempt to comprehend all of this.

Did that really just happen? Did I just make a dream date with a guy, the guy, that effortlessly? Yes, girl, yes you did. Nadine is going to lose her shit. I cannot tell her until later. Like, after I get home and do my victory dance in my pajamas to Prince's "If I Was Your Girlfriend."

"You know, this was originally recorded by Bobby 'Blue' Bland?" Anthony says rhetorically, as a heavyset woman belts out "Ain't No Love in the Heart of the City."

"Who? I thought it was Jay-Z, and Jaguar Wright collaborated on the unplugged version."

"Impressive reference, but no. Jay-Z just sampled it. If you like hip hop and R&B, there's a lot I could teach you about their origins in the blues."

"I'd like that," is my understatement of the conversation.

"Anyway, we should bring over a new bottle before your friends wonder what happened to us."

After the bartender pops the cork on our third bottle of the evening, I gather the frosty bucket and my glass from the bar, and Anthony removes my fox fur from the seat back. Leading the way to where my friends are sitting, my body tingles and my head spins slightly from the sensation of his fingers gracing my back. The feeling, like the man, is as real and sobering as it is surreal and intoxicating.

"About time, people could die of thirst around here," Nadine remarks as I set the bucket down in the center of the aluminum table.

Anthony pulls a chair out for me to sit, and I cannot look Nadine in the face as I respond, "Sorry, we were just talking shop."

After filling all but one glass, I raise mine in Lori's direction and make a toast, the meaning of which can only be fully understood by me. "To old friends and new beginnings." We clink glasses, and I down half of mine, hoping to drown the butterflies that are flitting back and forth between what just happened and what is about to happen.

Three poets, two singers, and one comedian – who might be funny but I am too preoccupied to know for sure – later, the emcee finally calls my name. I imagine my friends look shocked and are cheering me on, but all I can see is the dark, half-moon shaped stage and all I can hear is the *click, click, click* of my stilettos echoing against the cement floor.

I ascend the stairs and step into the only triangle of light cast from the pedestal barn light above. The deejay stops the music, I think it was Groove Theory's "Tell Me," as I regain consciousness and move the small black stool out of the way with a loud scrape. The thin microphone stand and I are alone here in this space, before a sea of muted faces, their features discernible for a brief second when a camera flashes. My hands do not shake like I expect them to as I unfold the paper from my jeans pocket and bend forward to speak into the microphone.

"Hello, I'm Athena Wallace, and I'm a columnist for *The Manhattan Socialite*. I'm doing a review tonight on Prose, and also writing a piece about a person who comes here... That person is me. If you don't mind, I'd like to share an excerpt with you."

After a slow, deep breath, I begin to read.

Among other things, some that even contradict one another, I am a writer, a daughter, a friend, a recovering perfectionist, and a terrible cook. I am clumsy and awkward at times. I over think everything except for what I really should, and am terrible with technology. I love fashion, a good bargain, cocktails, music, reality TV, and, most recently, myself.

Six weeks ago, I was assigned the task of documenting how people spend a night out in New York as a part of this best-of series. I was to dig into their personal lives and expose their most human qualities, uncovering the souls that give life to our city. Yet in the process of telling the stories of the five extraordinary individuals I met, something else happened, too: I uncovered a piece of my own soul. The piece I was beginning to think didn't exist, that I would never be complete without. The piece that held my happiness.

You see, my whole life I tried really hard to be the best at everything, and have the best of everything, because I thought that's where happiness comes from. As it turns out, it doesn't. Instead, I learned, happiness comes from belting out the song that love inspired you to sing. It comes from expressing yourself, as many versions of yourself that there are, completely and fabulously. It comes from chasing your dreams, stripping yourself naked and wearing your talent for all to see. It comes from persevering, regardless of the darkness of your past, and appreciating every single thing that you have. Above all else, it comes from living every day like it's your last.

So, to all of you, to all of the souls of the city who live with passion and purpose, thank you for everything. And to those souls who are struggling to find their missing piece, know that it's right there in front of you. Sitting next to you on the subway or driving your cab. In a piece of art displayed at the Met or on the graffittied walls of this metropolis.

It is in the words of a conversation that has yet to be spoken. Amidst your deepest fears and greatest desires. All you have to do is look up from your routine and notice; all you have to do is open yourself, your beautifully flawed self, to the new experiences your journey inspires. For happiness in life -- real, raw, stinging, sublime life – lies just outside of your usual.

About the Author

Cori Tadrus was born and raised in Syracuse, NY. She has a Bachelor of Arts degree in Anthropology from Syracuse University. She spent most of her twenties working as a refugee case worker by day and a bartender by night. Although passionate about this work, at the age of 30, she decided it was time to get a 9-5 job that paid the bills and did not require so much of her time and heart. She pursued a career in finance but it left her feeling empty and uninspired. She found respite in writing a story about a character named Athena who, like her, was seeking a more fulfilled life.

A few years later, Cori married an active duty Army Officer. When she was nine months pregnant with her daughter, she left her job to join him in his travels. With change came perspective, and the ability to look inside of herself to discover what she truly wanted to be: an author. When she is not writing, Cori enjoys mixing and drinking cocktails, listening to spoken word poetry and soulful music, impromptu dance parties with her daughter, and eating dessert.

CPSIA information can be obtained at www.ICGtesting.com
Printed in the USA
LVOW08s1816300516

490425LV00001B/41/P

9 780984 598625